Almost Doesn't Count

Almost

Doesn't Count

Electa Rome Parks

 New American Library

New American Library
Published by New American Library, a division of
Penguin Group (USA) Inc., 375 Hudson Street,
New York, New York 10014, USA
Penguin Group (Canada), 90 Eglinton Avenue East, Suite 700, Toronto, Ontario, Canada
M4P 2Y3 (a division of Pearson Penguin Canada Inc.)
Penguin Books Ltd., 80 Strand, London WC2R 0RL, England
Penguin Ireland, 25 St. Stephen's Green, Dublin 2,
Ireland (a division of Penguin Books Ltd.)
Penguin Group (Australia), 250 Camberwell Road, Camberwell, Victoria 3124,
Australia (a division of Pearson Australia Group Pty. Ltd.)
Penguin Books India Pvt. Ltd., 11 Community Centre, Panchsheel Park,
New Delhi - 110 017, India
Penguin Group (NZ), cnr Airborne and Rosedale Roads, Albany,
Auckland 1310, New Zealand (a division of Pearson New Zealand Ltd.)
Penguin Books (South Africa) (Pty.) Ltd., 24 Sturdee Avenue,
Rosebank, Johannesburg 2196, South Africa

Penguin Books Ltd., Registered Offices:
80 Strand, London WC2R 0RL, England

First published by New American Library,
a division of Penguin Group (USA) Inc.

NEW AMERICAN LIBRARY and logo are trademarks of Penguin Group (USA) Inc.

ISBN 0-7394-5564-8

Set in Bembo with Chalet
Designed by Daniel Lagin

Printed in the United States of America

This one's for Brandon and Briana, when you're older.
I only hope that you'll find your passions early in life.
For now, know that Mommy's loving you with all she has!

Acknowledgments

Today is a cold, wintry and rainy day in Georgia; one of those days when you don't want to venture out unless you absolutely have to. Outside is dreary and you can feel winter quietly settling in. Images of sitting in front of a warm fireplace, sipping hot tea and reading a great book come to mind.

As I sit in front of my PC, with sticky notes and affirmations all over the place, my house is quiet and still because hubby is at work and my children are in school. So . . . there is a serene, peaceful and calming presence all around me; I feel it, welcome it and embrace it.

The last few days, I realize and regret how much I've complained because I had to pay out a lot of unexpected money on my car. An Infiniti that has almost 200,000 miles on it. Yes! I drive my cars until they won't run any longer (LOL). Then, our five, six-year-old TV went on the blink. One minute it was working and then nada. It has been one thing after another. Did I mention, my car key broke off in the lock? Can you say locksmith and fifty dollars? Yet, sitting here this morning and taking the time to stop, reflect and really listen to my spirit, I realize how blessed I truly am. I'm too blessed to be stressed.

My New Year's resolution (this one I will keep) for 2005 is to continue to rid myself of negative people and their negative energies. I don't need to surround myself with people who want to block, downplay and diminish my blessings. I gravitate to people who are positive and encouraging and who are dream supporters, not dashers.

In reflecting, I realize I already have such a wonderful group of family, friends and associates that are supportive and I believe in giving people their flowers while they are alive and well. So here goes . . . The following people have played a special role in my life, have touched my heart, and enabled me in some form or fashion to realize my dreams.

Special thanks to:

First of all, I always give God the glory for allowing me to follow my dreams and achieve them. I realize all things are possible through him who strengthens me. Amen.

My husband, Nelson, and my children Brandon and Briana, you guys mean the world to me even when you're getting on my last nerve (LOL). I can't picture life without you and knowing that we chose each other when we were just a mere "thought" makes it all the better. And Briana thanks for telling me that if you had to choose moms all over, you would still choose me.

Tresseler Rome, thanks for continuing to be a fierce cheerleader in my corner and providing constructive feedback. I know I can always depend on you to keep it real! And thanks for the inspiration in *Almost Doesn't Count* where Mercedes and Shaneeka jack up Jamal's house. Hmm, I'll let you explain that one (LOL).

Laymon Taylor, DaJuan Crooms and Jordan Rome . . . you nurture me with your unconditional love. Enough said.

Sharron Nuckles, girl, I appreciate your putting up with me when it seems like the one and only thing I can talk about is books, mainly my books, and the publishing industry. I know the last couple of years haven't been the best for you health and employment wise; don't fret, things will get better. Even though you are feeling it and want to say, "Shut up already", you don't. We can be talking about a sale at our favorite store or ice cream and somehow I start to talk about my books (LOL). Give me some time; eventually my single, tunnel vision will fade

Tonia Davis and Tracy Craig, thanks for continuing to spread the word for me; it means a lot. Word of mouth is amazing. And Tonia, can you say *(I'm whispering now)* the psychic? *Inside joke (LOL).*

To my family members, you know who you are, thanks for the love and support. A special shoutout to my cousin, Talvin. Talvin Rome. Remember that name because he is going to do great things with his poetry (smile)! Just watch and see. This is a talented brother.

To my agent, Marc Gerald, thanks for believing in me from the very beginning. You are amazing. And you know, I always tell you, this is just the beginning of much bigger and better things to come. I'm claiming it!

To my editor, Kara Cesare, you are a class act. Thanks for guiding me along this new and exciting path. Your expertise is invaluable.

To my publicist, Mardessa Smith of Jadis Communications, Inc., we survived another literary campaign that places me even closer to the next level. Thanks for the added perks of being a friend and keeping me in stitches as well.

To the bookstores and book clubs, your support is greatly appreciated and highly valued. Without you, I don't know where I'd be; you constantly put the word out and hand-sell my books. Special thanks to the independent Atlanta bookstores: Medu (Nia), Nubian (Marcus), The African Spectrum (Nzenga), Oasis (Fanta),

B's Books and More (B'Randi), the Shrine of the Black Madonna (Amir) and Chapter 11 (Suzanne).

Black Expression Book Club, Nubian Sistas Book Club, Read-incolor Reviewers, Peoplewholovegoodbooks, Nghosi Books and Mahogany Book Club, just to name a few, thanks for your support.

Also special thanks to Heather Covington, C&B Books Distribution (Carol and Brenda), Rawsistaz (Tee) and Booking Matters magazine (Shunda and Jamill). Authors: Kendra Norman Bellamy, Sybil Barkley Staples, Tina Brooks McKinney, Maseyree, Kenny Blue and Sharon Rae, thanks for the camaraderie.

To my growing readership base: I love you guys (big hugs and smooches)! Thanks for the letters, e-mails and positive support; keep 'em coming. Please continue to share your feedback and keep me on my toes. Remember, I'm sensitive now (smile).

Until our next journey together, take care and be blessed.

Signing off (Atlanta, January 14, 2005: 11:16 a.m.) (*on my way to drink some hot tea*) . . .

Much love,
Electa

Prologue

*A*s the fresh, clean soapy smell of a recently bathed and lotioned body permeated and lingered in the small, cluttered bedroom, the young child lay flat on her stomach as her long, brown, slim legs carelessly dangled in the air. She ever so gently gave her baby doll, Sweetmouth, a plastic bottle of pretend milk.

The child had on her new pair of blue and pink pajamas with the cuddly kitten design that her mama had bought her, on sale at Kmart, after she begged and pleaded for them. She had even promised to be very good for an entire week. The girl's long, thick braids had already been greased, combed, brushed and tied down with a purple cotton scarf for the next day at school. She was an average, third-grade student at East Shoals Elementary School. Her favorite subject was math.

These were the moments she cherished, relished even. The child allowed herself to softly exhale out of her half-open mouth as she turned onto her back, got comfortable and stared at the ceiling with the dirty, chipped and peeling white paint. On quiet nights like this one, when all was calm and tranquil in her eight-year-old world, she allowed herself to dream. Dream happy thoughts.

Her mama was in the small front room, gossiping on the phone, laughing loudly, as usual, to her host of friends and "acquaintances," as she called them. Even as sleep tried to play captive to her heavy, drooping eyelids, the child continued to hug Sweetmouth within the arched cradle of her thin, brown arms, arms that bore the small scars of being an adventurous, curious and tomboyish child.

Sweetmouth was her best friend in the entire world. When the darkness came, with Sweetmouth nearby, the child didn't feel so afraid and alone. She told Sweetmouth all her deep, dark secrets in the wee hours of the night, whispered truths. Sweetmouth knew that sometimes the darkness brought the presence that did bad, ugly things to little girls. Things that made them feel dirty and bad, filthy and unclean.

The young child held on tighter to Sweetmouth and inhaled, even savored, the stillness and quietness of the night. With her right thumb in her mouth, she waited. She waited.

One

"Damn! That was sooo good, unbelievable," I shouted, basking in the afterglow of some off-the-chain lovin'. "Made my toes curl and shit." My body was still trying to claim and relish the last remnants of that delicious feeling like a crack addict trying to hold on to her last high. My plumbing would be good to go for at least another week; then it would be maintenance time again. However, I had another plumber in mind.

I had already scoped out this new guy at work. Dude was tall, dark chocolate like a Hershey's candy bar and wore at least a size twelve shoe, just like I liked 'em. I am not going to front and act all prim and proper. I craved myself some good lovin'. I keep it real. Some people enjoy a nice glass of wine after work or maybe a few puffs on a cigarette or cigar to relax. For me, sex—a good fuck—relaxed me. Took the edge off. Sex made me forget my worries for the moment. Gave me a natural high.

As much as I couldn't stand his crazy ass half the time—no, make that most of the time—Raheim knew how to throw down in the bedroom. In the kitchen. In the living room. Hell, even in the bathroom. Had a sista walking crooked the next day with a big Kool-Aid smile on her face and an occasional orgasmic flashback and twinge that made her pause for a moment. I had enough good sense to realize that was the only reason I tolerated his ghetto, ignorant, gold-tooth, thug-ass, drug-dealing self.

As I glanced over at him, sprawled on my new navy bedspread with a stupid grin on his face as he cupped his now-limp dick, my orgasmic high quickly faded. I wanted him out. Now! I didn't care if it is two a.m. on a rainy Saturday morning.

I intended to enjoy my last few hours in the cozy apartment that I shared with my lifelong best friend, Shaneeka. Raheim had served his purpose. Well, now it was time for his ass to step. The sooner, the better. He knew you didn't get no cuddling, cooing and catering here. I didn't play that shit, not me. I had no need for any emotional attachments. Wham, bam, thank you, ma'am worked for me.

By noon, I planned to have completed my drive down to south Georgia to spend the summer with my mama, Miss Betty, as she preferred for me and others to call her. Double damn. Miss Betty was another person who got on my last damn nerve after the first ten minutes. Sometimes after the first five. Yeah, she brought me into the world and shit, but you just had to know my mama to understand. She wasn't Clair Huxtable from *The Cosby Show*.

After a nasty fall at work, which damaged a ligament in her left leg, Miss Betty was recovering from knee and leg surgery and wouldn't be able to get around much for the next twelve weeks or so. Seeing how I was her only child—lucky me—I would play the role of her slave for the entire damn summer. My company, National Bank, was kind enough to transfer me to my hometown's banking center for the summer. Yeah right. Hell, I was doing them a favor. Who wanted to spend a hot-ass Georgia summer in, of all places, south Georgia? Someone not in their right mind. That's who. I grew up there and know the deal.

"Raheim!" I shouted, nudging him with my left foot.

He didn't answer, only lightly moaned and turned over onto his taut stomach. He looked like he was out for the count.

"Raheim. You gotta go, boo."

He still didn't move, so I kicked him this time. No, not hard. Just hard enough.

"Shit. Mercedes, what? What the hell do you want? Let me get some sleep, baby, and then I'll be ready for you again. Slow your roll for a minute."

"No, baby, you gots it all wrong. You ain't gettin' no more of this. Not tonight anyway. You gotta go," I said in true sista-girl fashion.

"Girl, you must be out of your damn mind if you think I'm gettin' out of this warm bed at two o'clock in the morning and driving halfway across town," he said, glancing over at the digital clock that sat on my nightstand, and then he rolled back over. Still laughing.

Oh no he didn't. "Raheim, get up!" I shouted, nudging him harder this time. "I mean it!"

"Mercedes, stop. You must have lost your damn mind! Girl, leave me the hell alone." He snatched and pulled the bedspread tighter around his muscular shoulders.

"Okay, okay fine. That's how you want to play?" I said, quietly and quickly edging myself out of bed and walking out of my bedroom. I was on a serious mission. "Two can play this game."

No, he didn't ignore me and tell me what he was going to do in my house! Oh hell no! I don't play that! I cursed to myself as I hysterically opened drawer after drawer in the darkened kitchen. I was so mad that my head was hurting right behind my eyes.

"Here it is. Let's see what his black ass has to say now."

I quickly walked down the hallway, back to my bedroom. Raheim was lightly snoring, unaware of what I had in store for his ass. He'll soon found out. He had known me long enough to know I didn't play. Female or male, it didn't matter. If you messed with me, you'd better be willing to get your ass kicked and served up.

As I tightened my grip on the wooden handle of the eight-inch butcher knife, I snatched the covers off Raheim in one swift, fluid motion. My favorite bedspread landed on the floor beside the bed. The moment Raheim opened his eyes to see what was going on, before he could utter one single damn word, I had the sharp tip of the steel blade pressed against his Adam's apple. For a flicker of a second, I saw fear in his eyes because he knew I was crazy enough to cut his ass. Yeah, I could be one crazy bitch if I had to be. Don't push me unless you wanted to be pushed back even harder.

"Now, what did I just tell you?" I was not even trying to hide my nakedness. I knew anyone peering in the bedroom window would have thought I was a crazed lunatic on the loose. With a crazed glaze in my eyes, I was looking wild with my hair all over the place as I raised the blade higher.

Raheim finally found the strength to talk. "Bitch, if you don't get that blade out my face, I'm gonna to beat your ass up and down this room. Don't make me go there. I promise you won't like the end result."

"No, you got it all wrong. You gonna get your black ass cut up in here. I'm not playin'. I'm not one of your lil' tricks."

Catching me off guard, Raheim quickly jumped up and tried to grab my right wrist, but I was too fast. By reflex, I grazed his Adam's apple with the steel tip of the blade. I immediately saw a trickle of red. His blood. A faint smile escaped my chapped lips.

"Damn! Damn! Damn! You crazy-ass bitch, I know you didn't just cut me," he screamed, making a sudden move in my direction. He wiped blood on to the back of his right hand.

For a moment, I was a little afraid. Just for a moment though. I knew Raheim's reputation on the streets. You didn't mess with him. But I didn't, couldn't, back down now. He'd have to back up his words. I started swinging the butcher knife back and forth, up and down, all around his face and balls.

"Call me a bitch one more time, you'll be the bitch up in here with no balls to claim. Once word gets out, see how much respect you get on the streets."

Raheim just looked at me with pure rage in his eyes.

"That's right. Come on. Try me. Yeah, try me."

"Bitch . . ."

"Did you hear me? Get the fuck out! Now!"

As he threw a pillow at me, Raheim somehow managed to get the bed in between us and continued to scream obscenities and rant and rave. That pissed me off even more. An internal rage erupted. A couple of seconds later, I was chasing his ass through my two-bedroom apartment, ducking chairs, throwing shit, screaming profanities, my breasts bouncing, his dick swinging, and telling him to get the fuck out.

I'm glad Shaneeka wasn't there to witness my latest outburst. But then again, knowing her, she probably would have looked at us, shaken her head and gone right back to bed and a deep sleep. Shaneeka had seen me in action before. Tonight she was over at her man's apartment.

Fifteen minutes later, I tossed the last of Raheim's clothes out my front door, and I heard him cussing as he struggled to find his dirty drawers, get dressed, and put on his new sneakers. Maybe he'd be able to get the bloodstains off them.

After rinsing off a few specks of blood, I carefully placed the butcher knife back in the kitchen drawer and slowly walked back down the hallway to enjoy the rest of my morning in my apartment. I didn't give Raheim a second thought. I had important things on my mind.

The little girl was suddenly awakened. Was that a noise she had heard? The girl strained her ears to hear. Nothing. She had long ago become a light sleeper. She pulled Sweetmouth closer into the cradle of her arm and smoothed down the doll's dark black hair. She dared not breathe. She waited for a sound. Strained to hear. Nothing.

As she cautiously and slowly raised her head up and peered into the pitch-black darkness, the girl anxiously held her breath. Fear had made small chill bumps appear up and down her thin brown arms. She shivered uncontrollably and pulled her covers tighter. Just as she was preparing to drift back off to sleep, she heard the sound again. Louder. Voices. Footsteps. As fear paralyzed her, Sweethmouth was crushed against her chest. If she were human, Sweetmouth would have heard the frantic pitter-patter of her heartbeat.

Two

"I'm gonna miss you, girlfriend," Shaneeka said in that whiny voice she sometimes used, the one I hated with a major passion. "What am I going to do the entire summer without you?" she exclaimed into the phone.

"I'm sure you and Jamal will manage somehow."

"See, girl, I'm trying to be serious. I am going to miss your stupid ass."

"Yeah right. Just don't let Jamal move in and take over. Keep him out of my shit."

"Now, you wrong for that. Anyway, I think he got some heifer on the side he screwing. He's always canceling our dates and disappearing for days at a time. Can't even reach him on his two-way. He won't answer his cell. I'd better not find out who the bitch is."

My roommate, Shaneeka, was Jamal's girlfriend. Jamal was a low-down dog, like most men I knew, had been for as long as I had known him. I didn't understand what Shaneeka saw in that loser, but evidently it was something, because he had been around, off and on, for almost five years, doing the same ol' BS. Personally, I didn't see any redeemable qualities in him. If it were me, I would have kicked Jamal to the curb years ago. I definitely wasn't Shaneeka. Jamal wouldn't step to me the way he stepped to her. No way in hell.

"I wouldn't be surprised and it wouldn't be the first or last time, Shaneeka. Why do you continue to put up with his shit?" I questioned, shaking my head slowly from side to side.

"Girl, everybody is not like you. Okay?"

"And what is that suppose to mean?"

"Girl, don't make me go there; I'll break it down for you."

"Yes, please do," I said loudly with much attitude creeping into my voice and my head bobbing from side to side with finger action thrown in for good measure.

"You know what I'm talking about 'Miss I don't need no good for nothing, low-down man. I can do bad all by myself. Miss I'm independent and can buy my own shit and a man can't do nothing for me but give me some. And better yet, if I have to, I can buy a toy and handle that my damn self too.'"

There was a moment of silence, then a series of small snickers filled the phone line. They started out small and elevated to a boisterous laugh. Minutes later, we were both laughing so hard that tears were rolling down my cheeks. I'd wipe them away and more would fall. Shaneeka had me, had me to a tee. I had quoted that motto many times. Too many to count.

We finally recovered enough to talk. "Oh no you didn't. Girl, you'd better be glad I'm your friend and I love ya like a sista. You got me, but I'm gone miss your crazy ass too. And I mean what I said about Jamal."

"Yeah, whatever! Call me when you get there and tell Miss Betty hello for me. Listen, try not to argue with her for at least twenty-four hours. You'd better be glad she can't walk or y'all would probably tear down the house this summer."

"Oh, you wrong for that too. By the way, there was some minor damage to some items in the living room. I'll pay for anything of yours that was accidentally broken."

"Jaheim?"

"Yeah, Jaheim."

"Are you okay?"

"I'm cool."

"Or should I ask, is he okay?"

"Let's just say Jaheim won't mess with me again."

"Girl, you're too bad. Drive carefully and call me when you get there; I should be home by then. I'm sorry I overslept and didn't make it over to see you off."

"Girl, I'm not gonna hate. I know Jamal put it on ya. And good. You probably couldn't even walk straight until this morning."

"And you know it. Bye, crazy."

"Peace, sweetie."

With a smile, I hung up the phone.

Forty minutes later, I entered the expressway with 97.1 blasting some of my favorite hip-hop songs on the radio. My Chevy was packed to the max with all my essentials for the long, hot summer ahead of me. I had packed plenty of shorts and, of course, work attire. I think I had brought every pair of shoes I owned. I was a shoe person—shoe freak to be exact. I'd buy one style of shoe in several colors if I caught a good sale.

I had to admit, I was definitely going to miss my girl. Shaneeka and I met back in first grade, found out we lived in the same low-income apartments and basically became inseparable through high school. We did everything together. Smoked, cursed and shared our adventures with men. After high school, I chose to go off to college, Albany State University on a scholarship, and Shaneeka went to beauty school.

Now, at thirty years old, we have reconnected. We are both un-married, have no children and are best friends as well as roommates. Over the years, we have been through a lot together. Some good and some bad. We have cried together and laughed together. Even acted like fools together. I just hate how Shaneeka allows men to use and abuse her. They walk all over her. I was there when she had her first abortion. The first of many. That girl uses abortions like it is a birth-control method.

Shaneeka is right, I can live without a man. I was actually celibate for a year, two years ago. Men are not special. Does a dick equate to special? I have seen too many bad relationships in my thirty years of living. I know you shouldn't judge all men based on a few bad apples. True. But . . . my mama, Miss Betty, taught me early on how not to choose a man. Whether she realized it or not.

Sadly, it's true. It's a man's world. Women are much smarter, but men know how to play the game to get what they want. They are results oriented. They just do it. Women bring too many emotions and hormonal shit into relationships. We got to analyze every damn thing. When good sex comes into the picture, women lose their damn minds. They think they own the man and got papers on him. Some women will put up with almost anything then, and the men really start tripping. I can't really blame men because they are only doing what we, as women, allow them to do. If he fucks you over once, guess what? He'll do it again.

So, years ago, I consciously decided I would get them before they got me. It wasn't a complicated decision to make; it was a natural step. Natural progression. I'm not searching for a soul mate in life. I realized a long time ago that I might never marry and have children. A man would have to be one hell of a man to get me to settle down, because settling is what you are doing. Losing part of yourself to be with him. A soul mate, that's the stuff fairy tales are made of, Lifetime movie-of-the-week crap. And love, what in the hell is love? I think it's a concept men came up with to keep women in check, to control women into wasting their entire lives searching high and low for this all-evasive love. Like some song used to declare, "Ain't nothing going on but the rent."

I've had a few friends and coworkers who thought they had found it—this all-evasive *love*. Look at Carol, this wannabee-bourge coworker of mine. I couldn't stand her fake ass. She wore a weave down her back and had green contact lenses. Carol met this fine-ass brother in a club, of all places. Clubs are simply meat markets. Places to legitimately hook up to screw. According to Carol, he swept her off her feet with flowers, romantic dinners, weekend getaways, the whole nine yards. A year later, they spent over forty-five thousand dollars, according to her, on a big fancy wedding. They invited everyone they had ever known in their entire lives and past lives. Went all out on the reception with a live band and open bars, etc. Everything was just beautiful. They had a European honeymoon. Perfect. Had sistas seeing the green-eyed monster, they were so jealous. They were smiling in her face and talking behind her back.

And then, two years later, Carol got a harsh reality check about this so-called thing called love. Unexpectedly, Carol arrived home early from work, didn't feel well, walked into their fancy-pansy bedroom, in their fancy-pansy three hundred thousand-dollar house and found hubby in bed with another man. Screwing each other's brains out. Get this, the other man was supposed to be her husband's best friend. Carol had eagerly accepted this other man into her home. He'd wined and dined with them. Was like one of the family. Where was love then? I guess her husband conveniently forgot about it when he was taking it up the ass. Carol is just bitter now. Yet she has a right to be, because the image of two big, strong black men going at it, in her bed, grunting and grinding, huffing and puffing, will never leave her. She even burned the bed.

But see, I am a grown woman, and myths and fairy tales have no

place in my world. I put love in the same category that I place Santa
Claus, the Easter Bunny, and the Tooth Fairy. Believe me, living with
Miss Betty shined a clear light on make believe and reality.

After readjusting and glancing in my rearview mirror for the
fourth time for the police, I checked my own reflection in the mirror. I'd been in such a hurry that I hadn't had time to put on my
usual Wet 'n' Wild brown spice lipstick that I usually bought at this
Korean shop out at South Dekalb Mall. Without it, I felt naked. It
complemented my chocolate complexion. I didn't have a blemish
to be seen. Unlike some dark-skinned sistas I know, I was proud of
my dark complexion. *The darker the berry, the sweeter the juice. Say it
loud! I'm black and I'm proud!*

As usual, Shaneeka had hooked my braids up. So I was set for
the long summer. I wore micro braids down to my shoulders because they were low maintenance. If I may say so myself, I was
looking kinda cute in my blue jean shorts that clung to my more-
than-ample butt like a second skin. And my crop top from Target
was showing just the right amount of 38C cleavage. Yeah, I am all
woman. Big butt, full lips and all.

I glanced over at the illuminated clock on the dashboard. It was
only a little after ten a.m. I was making good time. Traffic wasn't
bad. Just a few trucks on their way into Florida were on the highway. Before I knew it, I'd be greeting Miss Betty sooner than I was
ready to. I still hadn't prepared myself mentally. Yeah, you had to
prepare for Miss Betty and her verbal assaults. She had a way of
sneaking them in and catching you off guard. A stiff drink and a
dick helped. I took a couple of sips of my bottled, generic water
and switched stations as 97.1 started to fade. As I took my foot off
the accelerator because there was no need to rush, memories of the
past quickly flooded my daytime thoughts.

The little girl gulped for air to fill her straining lungs. In her efforts to hear and locate any foreign voices and noises, she had anxiously held her breath in anticipation.

There they were . . . again . . . if she listened carefully . . . the hints of hushed laughter that came after a few glasses of cheap wine or a few too many cans of beer that seemed to burst forth on weekends like new weeds invading a freshly mowed lawn in the summertime.

The girl's sense of smell was heightened, and she sniffed traces of the all-familiar potent and intoxicating cigarette smell. Weed.

She heard something or someone fall and make a loud thump on the living room floor. Hushed laugher followed. Intoxicated giggles. The little girl jumped. Trembled. With her eyes held tightly shut, so tight that tiny white spots danced behind her trembling, fluttering eyelids, she tried to will herself to sleep. Go to sleep, go to sleep, she silently repeated to herself. Even if it was only a temporary fix, sleep always made the living nightmares go away.

Three

I had exited off Highway 300, exit 99, and GA–FL Parkway on my way into Albany. It wouldn't be much longer now. I could do this trip with my eyes closed. "Long" and "boring" were two words that described it. Occasionally, a truck driver pulled up beside me, appreciated the scenery and honked his horn. In the past, depending on my mood, I'd give them a real show. Spread my legs, rub my nipples and stick my fingers under the flap of my shorts. I remember this one guy almost ran off the road. His old ass, should have been at home with his wifey instead of getting off watching me.

On impulse, I picked up my prepaid cell phone, which still had a few minutes left, to call an old acquaintance. After dialing the phone number from memory and letting the phone ring over ten times, I was about to hang up. I guessed Redman wasn't home. Too bad.

"Talk to me."

"Hey. What's up, boo?"

There was a small pause. I didn't know if my phone was acting up or not.

"Can you hear me? Can you hear me now?"

"Is this who I think it is?"

"Yeah it's me, Mercedes. What's up, baby?"

"It's all good, baby girl."

"I hear ya."

"What's up with you? Been a long time. Too long."

"Well, I'm staying with Miss Betty for the summer. She had some surgery, and I'm going to help out for a while."

"Well, my summer's looking better already. You know I got to check out your fine ass. When you dropping by? You know where I'm at."

"You reading my mind. That's what I was calling about. I'm not ready to go over to the house yet. I want to drop by for a while, catch up and just chill for a few. Is that cool?"

"Mercedes, you know you're always welcome here. You my girl. That's what I like about you. You moved out of the hood, got that good-ass job at that bank, but you still come back and kick it when you're in town."

"You know I could never forget you. You've always looked out for me. Still do. I'll see you in twenty."

Redman is one of the few men that I consider a friend. He is five years older, a very knowledgeable brother, but one who never used his intellect to improve his lifestyle. He still lives in the hood, smokes weed all day, works off and on doing construction-type jobs and still has that ghetto mentality. The white man owes him, so he says. Everything wrong in his life is because of the white man, so Redman lives off the state. We have kicked it off and on for years. That's what I like about him; his philosophy is no strings attached. That's right up my alley. We can handle things, get up, get dressed and not speak for months, and we don't catch feelings. We have an understanding. I like that. Like that a lot.

I made a pit stop at a service station to pick up two six-packs of beer. About twenty minutes later, I pulled up at Redman's apartment. Nothing had changed. This could be the projects in any city in America. The poorness hung in the air like a physical being; you could see the barely making it etched in the residents' eyes like an identification card. Invisible vapors of despair clung to the air like a heavy smog.

As always, loud, graphic, hip-hop music vibrated from a boom box where a group of teenage boys, all dressed in designer gear, congregated. The heavy, pungent smell of weed drifted my way and assaulted my sensitive nose. They turned in my direction to give me admiring stares, but on some level they knew better than to mess with me. I grew up in the hood. Over the years, I had learned how to turn my street smarts on or off. Now they were on. They knew I belonged. Was one of them. I'd been told that I carry a *"don't mess with me"* persona about myself. People learned to take me or leave me.

As I walked up the dirty, musty stairway, day-old smells of collards and fried chicken drifted my way. Collards and fried chicken, the food of the poor folk. It reminded me that I hadn't eaten lunch yet. On cue, my stomach growled. The smell of wine was heavy in the air. A permanent smell. I could hear a baby crying in the apartment next to Redman's. On the other side, angry voices filled the air. Harsh words and brutal slaps were exchanged. I knocked on his apartment door and said a silent prayer, thankful that I had escaped this, my old home in the projects. This was another world.

The door opened. "Baby girl! Come in and give me a hug."

We hugged and I felt his solidness. There was no strangeness here. I felt like I was back at home. Like I was welcome. I felt my tension take one step back. Then two.

"Let me look at your fine ass," he said, holding me back at arm's length.

As his eyes took me in, I saw his desire filter through for a split second. Men can be read so easily, and that's why they get caught in their shit all the time. Redman wanted some. His real name is Tyrail, but he has so much red in his skin tone that during the summertime he'll literally look red.

"You looking good, girl. I always was a sucker for a big butt and a smile."

"Thanks, I guess. And what is this?" I asked, playfully running my hand through his bushy, thick hair. "You trying to grow out your hair for an Afro?"

"No, this is the end result when you haven't made it to the barbershop in a few months."

We both laughed, a comfortable laugh between friends, as we took a seat on his sofa, the same sofa that I had sat on many times in the past. Lumpy, stained and barely hanging on. The TV was on a morning talk show. Montel Williams was taking questions from the audience for psychic Sylvia Browne. She had just told a mother the name of the man who murdered her twelve-year-old daughter.

"Boy, get me a comb and some hair grease and let me do something to your jacked-up head."

"Jacked up?"

"Yeah, you heard me right. Jacked up."

Redman obliged and returned with the requested items. He sat down on the floor, between my legs, and I began to comb out the tangled mess on top of his head.

"Hey. Take it easy. You know I'm tender headed!"

"Man, be still so that I can untangle this mess. When was the last time you combed this bird's nest? Last year?"

"Ouch girl! Damn!"

"Girl? Where you see a girl at?"

"My bad, my bad. You right. You all woman."

We had repeated this scenario many times over the years. As I slipped back in time, to my past, I felt my anxiety about Miss Betty easing into the recesses of my mind. Somewhere during this ritual, the beer managed to be opened and consumed. I took a few puffs of Redman's weed and caught up on the happenings in the hood. Like I said, not much had changed. Different names, but the same ol' shit. Same ol' drama.

As I finished the last neat row of cornrows, I was feeling pretty mellow and ready to face Miss Betty. Hell, I was ready to face anybody. Thanks to my handiwork, Redman had transformed back to his usual handsome self, and I was suddenly in the mood for a quickie. I touched him between the legs to let him know what was on my mind.

We did it silently and somewhat urgently. There wasn't much foreplay involved; with my shorts pulled down to my ankles, he was inside me with one quick thrust. Dry thrusts. My top wasn't even off. Redman had pulled me to the edge of his sofa, and I felt each and every thrust as he went in and out of me, deeply. He hadn't forgotten that I liked long, hard thrusts. I closed my eyes and wrapped my hands around the back of his head. I was wet now. It was running down my leg.

He flipped me over, took me from behind. I was on my knees with my butt in the air. It felt delicious as he palmed my butt with his large hands and gave all of himself to me in long, forceful thrusts. Yes, he knew how to make it hurt so good. *Hurt me, baby.* Right as I was about to reach my peak, we changed positions again so that he could suck my large breasts. That was a huge turn-on for me. My breasts are very sensitive. All the sucking and fucking sounds took us both over the top, and we collapsed onto each other, halfway on the sofa that had seen better days. I redressed and said my good-byes, while thinking how a good fuck could do wonders. I promised that I'd visit again. Yeah, I needed some more of that. Real soon.

Four

As I checked my rearview mirror to back out of my parking space, I realized it was time to face Miss Betty. I couldn't put it off any longer. Don't get me wrong. I love my mama. Really I do. At least, most of the time. We just have our issues to deal with, problems that over the years we haven't worked out. Our issues are like the black sheep of the family, kept at arm's length, never talked about and held as deep, dark, whispered secrets.

Miss Betty used to always say I had an old soul, like I'd been this way before. I have a sense of wisdom relating to lessons about life and living that are beyond my thirty years. I also know what I am and am not. No illusions come with me. I am not a pretender. What you see is what you get. Plain and simple. I am not looking to impress anyone or become anyone's best friend. I just want to live my life to the best of my ability and find happiness or some resemblance at some point along the way. So far, happiness is fleeting.

The short drive over didn't take more than fifteen minutes. As I turned off the ignition, I thought back to the last time I was home. It was over four months ago. Miss Betty and I had had words.

Looking at the small, modest brick house with the screened-in front porch, tiny front yard with the small garden on the side of the house, brought back many, many memories. Miss Betty and I had

moved in after Big Mama passed away when I was in the third
grade. It was the beginning of a new life for us; the house was the
one solid fixture that Miss Betty owned. Yeah, that house held a lot
of good and bad memories. If only I could deal with the bad.

I couldn't wait to move out and be on my own after I gradu-
ated from high school. I did just that and never looked back.
Everybody said that Miss Betty and I were too much alike—too
headstrong and set on getting our way. So many times along the
way we bumped heads like two male bulls defending their terri-
tory. To this day, we are still bumping heads.

While I retrieved my key to the front door, I managed to grab
a few bags out of the backseat of my car. It was now or never, I
thought, as I walked up the four crooked steps that led to the front
porch. I breathed in deeply and smelled the aroma of someone
cooking next door. Fried food, soul-food smells. Down-home
cooking.

Before I could even open the door all the way, the soulful
sounds of Al Green drifted out to temporarily take me back in
time. Miss Betty loved her oldies and played them often. She
owned a great album collection that consisted of some of the true
greats—The Temptations, Aretha Franklin, Al Green, Marvin Gaye,
James Brown, and Diana Ross and the Supremes; the records
would probably be worth something someday. Miss Betty always
said that that was real music. Not all this cussing, sampling, booty
shaking, no originality, that sold today.

When I was growing up, Miss Betty would have these house
parties on Friday or Saturday nights; actually, they were rent parties. The house would be full of liquored men and fast women
ready to let loose, have a good time and get their groove on. All
they had to do was contribute some dollars to our mortgage fund.
The monies were deposited into this big white shoe box that only

Miss Betty could touch. By the end of the night, the box would be stuffed to overflowing, full of dollar bills.

Sometimes the parties would last for two days straight. They'd start on Friday night and the partygoers would drift out on early Sunday morning to shower and make an appearance in church. Others had to be put out.

Back in her day, Miss Betty had a reputation around town of hosting a great party. The beer and liquor flowed freely. Whatever happened in Miss Betty's house, stayed in Miss Betty's house. The police were never called to settle disagreements.

I remember the air would be thick and heavy with the smell of cigarette smoke, and there would be ashtrays everywhere. There was always a game of tunk going on at that raggedly ass oak table she'd bring out and set against the far right wall. I remember one table leg was crooked, so the cards were always sliding halfway off. There was lots of talking shit and cursing. I just knew that Big Mama was turning over in her grave. But I have to admit, those parties kept the mortgage paid and hot food on the table when Miss Betty was between relationships and jobs. Sometimes her relationships were her job.

And the drama, it never failed that some wife or scorned girlfriend came up in there and busted her man holed up in the corner with somebody they weren't supposed to be holed up with. I think that's when I started seeing men for what they really are. Dogs.

I called out over the music, "Mama. Miss Betty, I'm here. Where are you?" I shouted, sitting my overnight bags near the front door and looking around.

The lights were off in the house, and the only light filtered in from the open miniblinds and sheer curtains that allowed the afternoon sunlight to shine brilliantly through.

I still didn't hear anything but Al Green singing about love and happiness. Then I pictured him with scalding grits on his back. Not a pretty picture. I called out again as I slowly walked towards the narrow hallway.

"Okay, okay, hold your horses girl. I heard you the first time," Miss Betty shouted, wheeling herself efficiently down the hallway. Other than the bandaged leg and the flowery housedress she wore, Miss Betty didn't look sick and weak from her surgery. She had the same old attitude and scowl on her dark face.

"Hey, Miss Betty. I see it didn't take you long to figure out this wheelchair and how to get around," I said, leaning down to give her a hug.

I felt her body tense and pull away within seconds. Her hands stayed at her sides. No return hug for me. It didn't matter that she hadn't seen me in four months. Hugs were a luxury in my household. They were rationed out in small doses, if at all.

"You got that right. I wasn't about to sit and stare all day at the four walls in my bedroom. Hell, that'd drive me crazy. Shit, this wheelchair is getting old already too. You know I don't stay still."

"Well, I'm here now, for the entire summer. So you take it easy and let everything heal properly. Remember what the doctor said." I had called and talked with her doctor, Dr. Miller, on several occasions. And I didn't want to have to stay longer than necessary.

"Child, don't come up in here trying to tell me what to do. I'm fine now; you should have been here a week ago."

"Miss Betty, you know I couldn't get away last week because of my job. They had to complete the paperwork for my temporary transfer, and I had to tie up some loose ends. I explained all that to you."

Miss Betty just huffed as she rolled herself into the kitchen, as if to dismiss me. She pulled open the refrigerator and peeked in and then closed the door. Didn't take anything out. I guess she needed to act busy.

"Didn't Mrs. Ferguson take care of you last week like I asked her to? She was suppose to cook your favorite meals, clean for you and help you get dressed and undressed. I even wired her some money in case you needed something. Last week, you told me you were fine when I talked to you on the phone," I said, walking into the kitchen.

"Mercedes, you know I don't trust that old bat farther than I can throw her. I want you to take a look around and let me know if any of my shit is missing. And if it is, when I can get up out of this chair, I'm going to go next door and kick her black ass up and down this street."

As she rolled over to the stove, I shook my head behind her back. My mama hadn't changed, not one bit. She is a big boned, dark-skinned, feisty lady who doesn't take no shit. From anyone. If she wasn't so mean, she could be considered fairly attractive for her age.

"Well, I'm here now. Let me get the rest of my things out the car and then I'll fix your lunch. I know you must be hungry by now."

I felt her eyes boring into me, taking me in from head to toe. Critical eyes. Harsh set of her lips. Head cocked to the side. Miss Betty was always sizing somebody up.

"Looks like you've put on some weight. Your butt is spreading."

"Not that I know of."

"Looks like it. Better start doing some exercises. Walking."

This time, I didn't even bother to respond. Miss Betty had a way of getting under my skin, one of the few people who could. And I refused to get started today. She was the one who didn't look like she had missed any meals lately.

"You any closer to having me some grandbabies?"

"Excuse me?"

"Girl, you heard me. You ain't deaf."

"Making a baby isn't on my to do list."

"Hell, what you waiting for? You definitely ain't getting no younger. You'll be thirty-one years old next year. You don't want to look like Sarah Ross's daughter; looks more like the grandmama than the mama. And the baby, bless her heart, looks like a lil' old woman too. I don't want no old-looking grandbabies that came from some old sperm and old eggs."

I had to laugh at that one because I'd seen the Ross baby and she did look like an old lady. Poor thang.

"Miss Betty, I told you, I may never marry. I ain't looking for no man."

"Shit, what lady doesn't want to marry and settle down? I may not have done it legally, but I always had somebody in my life, our life."

"I know. That was the problem. Someone was always around," I muttered under my breath.

"What did you say?"

"I'm going to get the rest of my bags out the car."

"Mer, did you hear me?" she called out. I kept walking. Okay, here we go again.

"Mer?"

Mer was my childhood nickname. As she called my name two more times, I kept walking right out the door. I thought to myself, it was going to be a long, hot summer. Nothing had changed. That was the one constant. Miss Betty and I still mixed like oil and water.

There. There was that sound again. Barely audible, but apparent neverthe-less. The little girl's body tensed up in anticipation. She knew it, sensed it. Yet each time it happened, she was always taken by surprise. The surprise making the event fresh and new, like the first time. The footsteps were get-ting closer. Coming down the short, narrow hallway. Stopping. Taking their time. Not in a hurry. Drawing out her fear. Stopping at her half-open door. She could sense the presence that peeked in with sinister, evil thoughts. Its dark aura immediately claiming its place in the small bedroom.

As she feigned sleep and quietly but quickly pulled Sweetmouth closer, she knew what would happen next. She prayed that it wouldn't happen again. She tried to always be on her best behavior and to do what her mama said—be respectful and get good grades. Yet this night, and many like it, had repeated itself over and over many times lately. She was caught up in a living nightmare with no escape.

Cuddled in each other's arms, the young girl and Sweetmouth anx-iously waited.

Five

"I'm serious, Shaneeka, they are sooo ass backwards down here," I cried into the phone, detailing my first week back home and at work.

"Girl, it can't be as bad as you describe it. Couldn't be. Remember I used to live there too."

"Believe me, it's probably worse. I'm the only black face in the place except for the janitor who cleans up at night."

"Umph."

"And I feel like some of my new coworkers resent my title. It's just as high, if not higher, than theirs."

"You're an assistant vice president in customer service, right?"

"Yeah." I was very proud of that accomplishment.

"You go girl."

"I even heard one coworker, Jennifer, talking about me behind my back to another associate."

"Damn, you kidding!"

"Yeah, girl, that fat heifer was laughing at my name. Said what mother in her right mind would name her child Mercedes, after a car that she'd never drive a day in her life because she couldn't afford it. Said I was straight ghetto underneath my facade of cheap business suits and heels."

"Damn!"

"Is that all you can say?" I asked in growing irritation.

"Now, Mer, you should be used to that joke by now. There are not too many women named Mercedes Lexus Jackson. At least your last name isn't Benz."

"I know. We can say that, not them. That's the difference. I can't explain to them that Miss Betty named me after her favorite cars because Mercedes and Lexuses are powerful machines, and she wanted me to grow up and become a powerful woman. And her dream was to own a black Mercedes and Lexus."

"What was your mama thinking?"

"I don't know. I ask myself that each and every day."

"Well, I wouldn't sweat it. Which I know you aren't. Look at it this way, you're only there for the summer."

"Amen to that. Thank goodness."

"Amen. I hope you don't kick somebody's ass up in there. I can see it now on the local news: Local woman goes crazy inside bank and kicks coworkers asses! Details at five o'clock."

"Girl, you just don't know. I have to grit my teeth to keep from commenting some days. They just don't know. Let 'em keep on messing with me. I'm gonna show them just how ghetto I can get."

We both laughed at that because we know I'm not lying.

"What's going on with Redman? Because I know you've hooked up with him."

"That's scary. Girl, you know me too well. But he's still laying it down in the bedroom like I like it. He still got that magic stick, girl. Thick and long. Other than that, he's still the same. Living off the state. Content to get high every day."

"What's up with Miss Betty? Did you tell her I said hello? How are the two of you getting along?"

"Will you ask one question at a time? Damn."

She just laughed. "My bad."

"Amazingly, me and Miss Betty are getting along okay. She's only made me pull out a few of my braids. Maybe I won't be bald by the end of the summer. It is kind of strange seeing her in a wheelchair. I've never seen her sick before. Still, I think this is the quiet before the storm."

"Yeah, well, the question is which one of you is the eye of the storm?"

"Ask me that in a few weeks."

"Yeah, if you make it that long."

There was a moment of silence. I switched the phone to my other ear.

"Girl, I found a silver hoop earring under Jamal's bed."

"For real? What the hell you doing under the man's bed?"

"Don't worry about all that. Anyway, he claimed it's mine."

"Well, is it? Damn girl, you don't know your own earring?"

"Jamal did so much smooth talking and double talking that he had me thinking it was mine."

"Ump!"

"When I got home and thought about it, I realized I haven't owned a pair of silver earrings in over a year. I haven't worn any since I bought a pair from that Atlanta street vendor and they broke out my earlobes."

"Sad. Shaneeka, you are a beautiful lady. You can get anybody you want. Why do you continue to put up with his BS?"

"Because I love him."

"Well, love ain't keeping him in your bed. Love ain't keeping him from disrespecting you every chance he gets. Love ain't keeping him from using and abusing you. Wake up. Smell the bullshit."

She didn't say anything.

"Listen, I have to go, girl, before this bill gets too high." I didn't tell her, but I really didn't want to continue the conversation about Jamal. Gave me a freaking headache.

"Okay then, love ya."

"Love ya back. And remember, I got your back."

As much as I loved my homegirl, she could seriously work my nerves. Shaneeka was gorgeous with her twists, smooth brown skin and big doelike eyes. I saw the looks men gave her when we went out to the clubs. Yet she only had eyes for Jamal.

Other men didn't exist for her. Too bad.

Six

It was a week later, a lazy Friday night. Miss Betty and I had settled into somewhat of a routine, if you want to call it that. I
cooked her a hot breakfast before I left for work each morning,
quickly came home for lunch to check on her and throw together some cold sandwiches and then we sat down for dinner
each night. I was becoming quite the cook. I enjoyed trying out
new recipes and ideas. During the daytime, Miss Betty relaxed by
watching TV, reading or completing her crossword puzzles. Oh,
let's not forget her favorite pastime . . . talking on the phone. It's
funny, other than being a little immobile, you'd never know
she'd just had surgery. Her surgery definitely hadn't changed her
disposition.

Work was a trip because my coworkers had some serious race
issues to resolve. Duh, this is the new millennium. Wake up. Your
ancestors don't own my ancestors anymore. I don't have to sit in
the back of the bus. However, the actual job responsibilities and
duties were no different from what I performed back home. Being
a Customer Service Representative III was the same everywhere.
People were people. Opening and closing checking and savings ac-
counts are my primary responsibilities. I also have to cross sell
products as much as I can, and I am required to research inquiries
that arise from customers. So thankfully that transition was simple

enough. I was not stressed over my move, and I refused to let my coworkers stress me out.

I finished washing and drying the dinner dishes and putting them up. Now I was bored out of my mind. I could actually hear crickets chirping outside the open front door, and it was hot as Hades up in the house. Miss Betty refused to turn on the air-conditioning after six o'clock in the evening. She claimed that this saved on her electric bill. Bottom line, we roasted like two pigs held over an open pit. I had stripped down to as few clothes as possible. Now Miss Betty was watching one of her favorite TV game shows. Give her some cigarettes, a couple of draft beers and she is set for a minute. For me, I'm not used to a Friday night with nothing to do and nowhere to go. If I were at home, it would be on. Decatur and Atlanta had plenty of hot clubs to party in. I wanted to get my groove on.

I glanced over at Miss Betty sitting near the sofa, totally absorbed in her show. I might as well have not been there. She had a knack for tuning people out, making them invisible. I didn't like to be ignored. My eyes traveled down to her hands. For a woman of her stature, she had rather small hands, almost delicate. You'd never know she had worked in various restaurants and a school cafeteria for most of her adult years. Her hands told a different tale.

"Miss Betty, your nails have seen better days. Chipped fingernail polish and hangnails? Let me hook you up. I brought my nail kit from home."

For a brief second or two, she turned away from her show and looked at me like I was up to something. Seconds later she was back into the program as if I'd never spoken.

"I'm not going to beg you. I don't think I've seen a day when your nails and hair weren't perfect. You slacking off." That was Miss Betty's major vice. She'd give her last penny for a manicure.

"Okay, but you'll have to wait until *Jeopardy* goes off. See, you made me miss the answer. That was the only one I didn't know."

"Yeah right," I murmured.

"My lawd, it's going to storm."

I looked at her with total confusion because the nighttime sky with its many shining stars was clear as far as I could see. Not a cloud in the sky.

"You volunteered to do something for me?"

"Miss Betty, I don't do nothing for you? I can't believe you said that; I'm here for you now."

"Yeah, you here. Only because a daughter is suppose to be here for her mama. You're here out of obligation."

"What about the money I send each month, the gifts I've bought you, the items I've purchased for this house?" I asked in utter amazement.

"What about them?" Miss Betty inquired.

"You know what? It don't even matter."

"Shh, I'm trying to watch my show. You made me miss the answer again."

"Whatever."

"You better watch that mouth. I'll get up out of this chair on one leg and show you who's who."

As I got up to go to my room, I was thinking, *Yeah, you'll get up, but your old ass will be beat back down in five seconds flat.*

I must have fallen asleep on my worn bed because I was awakened with Miss Betty calling out to me. At first, I thought I was having another one of my crazy dreams. I looked around in confusion.

"Mer!"

"Ma'am?"

"I'm ready for you to do my nails. Bring that pretty, bright red out here and paint my toenails too."

"Okay, let me find it."

"Come on, girl. Hurry up. I don't have all night."

Before I laid down, I was thinking of dropping by Redman's for a booty call. Ain't no shame in my game. But there's no telling who he had up in his place on a Friday night. Redman was known for messing with some wild women. I didn't want to start nothing I would have to finish.

Ten minutes later, I had set up nail polish remover, cotton balls, a file and nail polish on a makeshift dinner tray. Miss Betty was sitting in her wheelchair like she was Queen of the Nile or something. She was munching on some grapes and playing a game of solitaire.

I lifted her left hand and examined the thin veins, lines and a few, faint scars—her battle wounds. In my childhood, that hand had struck my butt many times as it dealt out spankings, some deserved and some not. I admit, I was always getting into trouble about something or other. I was a total tomboy and rebel.

We sat in an uncomfortable, awkward silence. Miss Betty and I were not used to sharing moments or just sitting and talking. Most of the time, when I visited in the past, I stayed in the streets. Miss Betty's was simply a place to rest my head.

"I'll probably need to go to the grocery store tomorrow," I said, breaking the silence.

Miss Betty, again, glanced up at me briefly, didn't comment and looked back down at her deck of playing cards.

"Go."

"Is there anything in particular that you'd like?"

"Food."

"Do you always have a smart answer for everything?"

"That wasn't smart, Mer. I answered the question you asked me."

I just nodded, determined not to let her upset me, and went to applying the first coat of red nail polish. What a freaking Friday night. I didn't know if I could handle this for the entire summer or not. What had I gotten myself into?

"What are you cooking for Sunday dinner?" Miss Betty asked.

"Food."

I didn't even look up, but I thought I saw her glance at me out of the corner of her eye. I could be a smartass too.

I finally finished Miss Betty's nails, and they looked one hundred percent better. Almost professional. I even combed and brushed her hair. I greased it like I used to when I was a child, and placed it back in her usual French bun. Even though I didn't comment, I noticed a few gray hairs that she usually kept hidden with a black rinse.

When I got up to leave with my supplies in hand, I noticed Miss Betty admiring her nails and hair in the handheld mirror I'd brought out from the bathroom. Vain ass. Actually, less a few pounds, Miss Betty was an attractive woman for her forty-nine years. She'd be fifty at the end of the year.

"Well, I'm calling it a night. Don't stay up too late, Miss Betty. You don't want to overdo it."

Silence. I kept walking.

"Mer?"

"Yes?"

"Thanks."

When I looked back in surprise, she was already into another show. Still munching on her seedless grapes. The card game was forgotten and placed to the side.

"You're welcome," I whispered, making my way up the short hallway to my childhood bedroom. Once I was finally showered, lotioned and tucked in bed, I wondered if Miss Betty and I would ever find our way back to each other. We had interacted like this for years now, blowing up at each other or walking on eggshells. However, I remembered when things were different, when we had a special mother-daughter bond. When did that change? And would we, if ever, get back what we had lost?

The girl felt the presence rather than actually seeing it. The presence that watched her as she slept, or pretended to sleep. As always, the smell of alcohol and cigarettes assaulted her nostrils first.

If she listened closely, she would swear she could hear the erratic breathing of the presence. Even though her back was turned, she could feel the piercing stare that she had become accustomed to.

The little girl wanted to move, shift position so badly, but she willed her body to remain still, perfectly still. Maybe, just maybe, the looming presence would go away. Maybe the presence would let her sleep and tonight would be different. Tonight she wouldn't have to huddle and tremble in fear, confusion and mental pain.

The girl wondered why the presence couldn't or refused to smell the fear that seeped out of her pores. The room was shrouded in fear. Then she knew, the presence grew stronger because of her fear. The girl wanted to call out to her mother, to scream for help and salvation from her tormentor. Yet no screams erupted from her throat. Her throat was dry and constricted. Only the silent screams played out inside her mind. Warnings about what her tormentor would do to her quickly came to mind. Any thoughts of screaming quickly vanished.

Seven

I knew it was only a matter of time before my good fortune with Miss Betty ran out. To be honest, aside from a few snide remarks and minimal conversation, Miss Betty and I had gotten along okay. Better than I had expected, anyway.

Even though Miss Betty would never, in a million years, admit it, I know she is sorta depressed. After all, Miss Betty has never really had to depend on anyone. Just as she has raised me to be, Miss Betty is a strong, independent woman. She has worked in the high school cafeteria for as long as I can remember. Even though the pay isn't that great, she has a knack for making a dollar out of twenty-five cents. Now she is temporarily out on disability. I know this has to be hard to deal with. Also, there are rumors of layoffs at the school, which is causing her additional stress.

Did I forget to mention she is very opinionated as well? Miss Betty was never one for holding back her sharp tongue; she speaks her mind without any regard for whose feelings she may hurt in the process. I'll never forget that Sunday morning when she waltzed into Bald Rock Baptist Church dressed to the nines from head to toe, had on a sharp red suit with a matching hat. She calmly and primly stood up in church and told off Reverend Nolley in front of his deacons, the mother board and his entire congregation, visitors and friends. Miss Betty spoke like she was a sailor on leave after being out to sea for several months. People still talk about that like it happened only yesterday. After she had her say, Miss Betty calmly walked down the aisle and out the front doors, never to set foot in that particular church again. However, that's another story.

During the day, when I was at work, Miss Betty talked to her friends on the phone. The phone was her third limb. In fact, during my second week back, she had had many visitors in and out of the house. They'd stop by, sit and gossip for a minute. From my bedroom, I could hear them just giggling, cackling and passing on the dirt about some unsuspecting soul. Telling on this person, swapping gossip, exchanging stories and loving every minute of it. That's how Miss Betty kept track of everybody's business in town.

However, Miss Betty was too quiet with me. Wasn't like her. I knew she was holding back so that we could cohabitate for the summer, or whatever her reasons were. For as long as I could remember, I was a disappointment to Miss Betty. I realized that and accepted it. She wanted me to share her opinions about life and living—I didn't. So we fought.

Eight

Saturday evening's argument didn't come as a surprise. I had expected it sooner. We were sitting in the living room in our usual spots, me on the burgundy-striped sofa that had seen better days. Miss Betty was beside the recliner, in her wheelchair. I was halfheartedly flipping through an old copy of *Ebony* magazine that had been lying on the coffee table since I had arrived home. Miss Betty was reading the local newspaper with the TV turned on again, as usual. I didn't think she could live without that TV and remote.

It was obvious that I was restless. After talking to Redman and hearing him describe in graphic detail what he wanted to do to me, I was horny as all get out. Phone sex didn't do it for me, only made me crave the real thing. I knew I had checked my wristwatch a few times. It was only a little after six p.m. When I was anxious or nervous or restless, I tended to shake my right foot back and forth. I had caught myself doing it several times already. I couldn't sit still.

Miss Betty broke the silence.

"Child, will you stop all that fidgeting over there? Be still. I see you haven't outgrown that annoying habit."

"I'm not fidgeting."

"Yes, you are. I know fidgeting when I see it."

"Well, maybe you need to put on some glasses."

"Mer, shut it up."

"Whatever," I whispered under my breath.

"Umph. Are you going somewhere? You've looked at that watch about ten times in the last fifteen minutes."

"Yes . . . No. I haven't decided yet."

"Mer, you don't have to babysit me. I've taken care of myself all my life. I think I can do it for a few hours. You're young. Go have some fun. Besides, you are getting on my nerves with all that damn fidgeting."

I didn't say anything. I just continued to flip through my magazine, not really seeing the pictures of who was hot that month. I did stop to admire the six-pack on LL Cool J. And those lips, God help us!

"I'm surprised you haven't made a beeline for that Redman with his trifling ass. Or maybe you have, knowing you. You need to stay away from him and his troublesome ways. I don't know why you and that friend of yours are always running after these good-for-nothing men."

"Here we go again. I don't understand why you don't like Redman. You never have. He has never disrespected you."

"Well, let me count it down for you. Number one, he's no good. Number two, he doesn't work. Number three, he's no good. Are those enough reasons?"

"Well, he's just an old friend, and I'm not trying to marry him or nothing."

"There you go. That's your problem. You're not trying to marry anyone. You're totally content hopping from bed to bed, from dick to dick."

"Miss Betty, I'm all the way in Decatur. You have no idea what I'm doing or whose bed I'm in."

"I do, 'cause I know you, and you haven't changed."

I closed my eyes. I inhaled through my nose and quickly counted backwards from ten to one. By the time I made it to three, I was much calmer. I no longer felt like a dragon breathing fire.

"I'll never forget that time—you were about sixteen."

"Oh lord, here we go again."

"I came home early from work—I had the flu—and caught your fast ass and Redman screwing like rabbits in the middle of my living room floor. Both of y'all butt-ass naked, and you, with your long legs wide open while he had his way with you. All that moaning and going on. And the smell of reefer was all in the air. Had to leave the windows up for a couple of hours to clear the air. Up until then, I still thought you were a virgin."

"And you never let me forget it, either."

"You're right, I didn't. I didn't want you to end up pregnant, on welfare and in the projects, with no future in this small, two-bit town."

"Like you did with me, right? I'm so sorry that your having me messed up your life. You know, I didn't ask to be born. Maybe you should have kept your legs closed as well."

"Mer, it's not even like that. I'm just saying that I wanted you to have a better life than I did."

"And I do, Miss Betty. Can't you see that? I went to college on scholarship, I have a stable job with the bank, I have my own apartment, my own car and I'm independent. I'm happy."

"Are you? Are you really happy, Mer?"

"Yes. Yes, I am."

"Sometimes I look at you, and I see a lost soul. Mer, you got to start thinking about settling down and having a family at some point."

"Well, I'm going to live my life the way I want to. You can't live your life over through me. Can't you accept that?"

Miss Betty cut her eyes at me and chose to simply ignore me, yet again. This time, I chose to confront her. I exploded. Overflowing like a volcano with hot lava that scalded to the touch.

"So what? I enjoy the company of a lot of men. I'm not doing anything men don't do every single damn day. Yeah, Miss Betty, I love dick and I'm going to get mine. Is that clear enough? And I'm not doing anything you didn't do when you were younger. At least I have a preference. Back in the day, you didn't care if you laid up with a male or female, married or not."

"How dare you! Don't you ever disrespect me like that again."

"Disrespect you? Disrespect you by stating truth? You disrespected yourself. I'm simply stating facts. You opened this can of worms. Do you really think I've forgotten all those men—my *uncles* you called them—and women—lets not forget my *aunts*—you paraded through here like an Easter parade down Main Street? I was a child, but I still had eyes and ears and feelings. Somewhere along the way you forgot that!"

"Child, I don't know who you think you're—"

"You talk about me and Redman. What child wants to walk in on her mama with her legs spread open, getting her coochie eaten by some woman from church who sung in the choir? I remember all that and more. Yeah, much more."

"Mer, back then we were living tooth to tooth, paycheck to paycheck. Hell, I still am. Anyway, I did what I had to do to survive. If a few of my friends wanted to help us out, let me borrow a few dollars, so be it. Your aunts and uncles kept food in your mouth and new clothes on your back."

"Spare me. You know what, Miss Betty? It doesn't matter. I just want you to quit placing judgment on how I choose to live my life.

I'm not hurting anyone, and I'm not sleeping with married men. Can you say that? Remember old man Johnson from around the way? As I recall, he was married with two teenage daughters. I had to see them every day at school. And every day they looked at me with accusing, black eyes. Because of you, they hated me. You turned him out and treated the poor man like a dog. You are not innocent, pure or without fault yourself. People who live in glass houses shouldn't throw stones," I proclaimed, feeling a serious headache coming on strong right behind my eye.

"Mer."

I held up my upturned hand in true ghetto-girl fashion. "I don't want to hear it. I'm not going to hear it. I'm not going to apologize for how I live my life. I've heard enough. I know who and what I am. And guess what? That's enough for me. If you think your daughter's a whore, well that's on you. The apple doesn't fall far from the tree," I literally screamed out in desperation.

I leaped up off the sofa and could feel her intense stare piercing my back as I made my way to the kitchen. I was pissed. Hell, I was beyond pissed. I knew if she said another condescending comment about me, I was going to go off and expose all our dirty secrets. And there were many. Most of the time they came out in my nightmares. I'm sure Miss Betty slept well.

"Where are you going?"

Between clenched teeth, I said, "I'm going to the Piggly Wiggly to buy groceries for next week." I had to get out of there. I couldn't stand being in the same room with her. I felt like the air was closing in on me. I couldn't breathe.

"Oh, well, grab my purse over off the kitchen table and look in there . . ." She said this like we hadn't had major words just five seconds earlier.

"No, Miss Betty. I have money. I'll buy the groceries. I wouldn't want you to say I never did anything for you. Mark this date and time on your calendar. Okay?"

I retrieved my purse and keys and headed out the door as quickly as I could. Only when my feet hit the street was I able to breathe again. I took quick gulps of air. Breathed in and out.

Nine

By the time I made it to the local Piggly Wiggly, which was about five minutes away, my breathing had returned to normal and my anger had subsided to a mild simmer.

For a Saturday evening, the parking lot wasn't that full of cars. That was a good sign, because I was not in the mood for trying to navigate a grocery cart up and down food aisles through a crowded store. Nor was I in the mood for long lines at the checkout. It would be my luck that I'd end up standing behind someone with a million coupons.

My plan was to purchase enough food for next week's meals, drop the food off at the house and head over to Redman's to take him up on his offer. And I knew he could deliver what I needed to take my mind off my problems. I needed just a few hours of relief and then I'd be all right.

Redman had been sexing me on and off for years; he knew what I was into. A lot of men didn't feel the sex games I liked to play. I definitely couldn't see myself spending the evening with Miss Betty. I'd had enough of her to last a year, hell two years.

I leisurely and efficiently pushed my grocery cart up and down the inside aisles; I always grocery shopped that way. I started with the inside aisles first and made my way to the perimeter areas last. In my haste to leave Miss Betty, I hadn't made a list or even checked to see what we needed. The store had a lot of good deals, like buy one, get one free, and other discounts, and I was checking them out. That's one thing about me, call me frugal, but I believed in finding a good buy. I didn't like to spend my money; I could spend somebody else's, but not mine.

I compared prices and didn't really pay attention to other people in the store or my general surroundings. My mind was a million miles away. Images of the scene at home kept flashing before my eyes like a bad movie. And I saw red all over again. I felt a mild throbbing between my eyes. I massaged my temples. At one point, I made it over to the dairy section, and I thought I could sense someone staring at me. You know the feeling.

I looked up slowly and to my immediate left. I found myself looking into the bubbling brown sugar, sexy eyes of an attractive, thirty-something cutie's face. He smiled, showing me his straight, white teeth. Perfect. I didn't smile back. I couldn't help but notice the dimple that stood out like a spotlight in his right cheek.

Instantly my ghetto mode kicked in, just instinctively took over. My mode said, "Don't fuck with me today; I'm not in the mood." I wasn't feeling it today, being picked up in a grocery store. Any other time, I may have been interested. The brother was fine in an unassuming, macho way. The stranger was a medium-dark-skinned brother, about five-ten or so, bald head, goatee, and very kissable lips. He licked his lips in an LL Cool J sorta way and looked back in my direction. For a minute, I had an image of what those lips and mouth can do to my kitty cat. I felt a warmness rising. Then I remembered that Redman was going to hook me up later.

Dude had on Sean John jeans, a button-down shirt, and white leather sneaks. I saw all this out of the corner of my eye as I picked up a gallon of milk. I checked the expiration date.

Dude was still trailing behind me, a few feet away. I knew he was checking me out from behind. I could feel his eyes boring into me as he focused on my ass. I put a little extra sway into my walk for good measure. I knew I had back. Hell, my ass was one of my finer assets. My hand immediately went to my hair. In my haste to escape Miss Betty, I didn't have on any lipstick either.

At one point he was right beside me. Dude reached across me to grab a carton of skim milk. His hand barely missed my breast. I didn't see a wedding band. That was good.

"Excuse me."

I didn't respond. Just pushed my cart farther down to the orange juice and eggs. I knew I needed to pick up a crate of some medium eggs for breakfast. Miss Betty loved eggs. Cooked sunnyside up and slightly runny.

"They have some good buys."

I didn't respond and secretly laughed inside. He didn't have a better line than that? No wonder he was alone on a Saturday evening. Tired-ass line.

By now, I was down by the meat section. Within seconds, cutie was coming my way. He had it going on with that strut. Reminded me of that famous Denzel Washington walk. Confident and manly. Whatever cologne he had on was doing him much justice too. I had caught a wisp of it when he reached across me.

"You look familiar. You live around here?"

I didn't turn around. I was totally focused on the twelve-piece family pack of chicken legs and wings. If I split them up, that could be enough for two meals. "No."

"A lady of very few words," he said half to himself.

"Excuse me?"

"I said, a lady of few words."

"Yeah, for you."

"Whoa, my bad. Baby got up on the wrong side of the bed this morning."

"No, baby didn't, and I'm not your baby by the way. Know that."

By now, we were face-to-face. He was even more attractive and sexy than I had given him credit for. His eyes were deep, dark and penetrating. The kind you could get lost in. Dude was looking at me like, "Whoa, what have I gotten myself into?"

"Listen, miss, I didn't mean to upset you. I was just admiring a pretty lady. That's all."

"Well, you should step to me like a man. Don't get up in my face with those corny one-liners or check out my ass and tits when you think I'm not watching."

He just looked at me like I had lost my damn mind. I thought I even saw the beginnings of a smile forming on his lips. That pissed me off big-time because he wasn't taking me seriously.

"You're absolutely right. I'm rusty. I've been out of the dating game for some time. Let me introduce myself. I'm Darius," he said, extending his right hand. I still didn't notice a wedding band on his large hands. That didn't mean anything though. Many married men didn't even wear a band anymore, and I was all too familiar with the "leaving it in the car" routine. I weaned one married man off of that trick. I called his wife. I told her everything. I didn't mess with married men, so don't step to me like you aren't—or suffer the consequences.

There was a long pause where I internally debated if I should give my name.

"Mercedes," I said with much attitude, but didn't extend my hand in greeting. Yeah, I left homeboy hanging.

I moved farther down to the pork chops and was picking up prepacked packages and reading the backs like they held the for-

mula for peace on earth and goodwill towards all. He followed behind me like a male dog following a bitch in heat. Not saying I'm
a bitch.

"Well, Mercedes, I was wondering if I could take you out to
dinner or a movie sometime? You seem like an interesting lady, and
I'd like to get to know you better."

"No, no thank you."

I could tell that threw him for a loop. He wasn't used to being
rejected. Women threw him a lot of play and pussy.

"No. May I ask why not? My breath stinks? One leg shorter
than the other? Do I have a cocked eye I don't know about?
What's the deal?"

Secretly, I kinda had to laugh at that one. I turned away so he
wouldn't see the beginnings of a tiny smile on my lips. I had to give
it to him. He was persistent. And if he weren't so cute, I would
have told him off by now. Cursed his ass out.

"I don't have to have a reason. I simply have a choice. And I
choose not to go out with you. I don't want to go out with you.
Period. Is that simple enough? Does that spell it out for you?"

"Okay, cool. You chose and I lost," he said, beginning to walk
away slowly as he shook his head in disbelief. He wasn't used to
women like me.

He stopped in midstride, paused and turned back my way.
"Wait, listen, there's something about you that's refreshing. You're
not like most of the women in this town. Can I at least get your
phone number?"

"No."

He smiled. I didn't.

"Okay, cool. Can I give you mine?"

"Sure, you can give it to me."

"Will you call me?"

"Maybe, maybe not. I don't know."

"Well, at least you didn't say no. That's a start."

I supplied the paper and pen. Dude wrote down his name and phone number on a sheet of torn paper and handed it to me. Darius Dargon. I took it, swiftly stuffed it into my purse and kept pushing my cart. I didn't look back.

He yelled, "Mercedes, I'll see you around, hopefully. Give me a call when you wake up on the right side of the bed."

I just nodded my head and kept right on pushing my cart. I could feel his eyes boring into my back until I turned the corner down by the rice and pasta aisle. I threw two boxes of brown rice into my cart and grabbed a box of Hamburger Helper on my way to the checkout aisles.

Fifteen minutes later, I had paid the teenage cashier who looked like she wanted to be anywhere but there, sixty-five dollars of my hard-earned money and put the groceries into the trunk of my car. Before I opened the driver's door to my car, I took the small sheet of paper that Darius had given me out of my purse, looked at it one last time, tore it up into teeny, tiny pieces. As I drove off, the pieces blew away into the humid, evening air. Forgotten.

The door inched open a little farther. The girl heard the familiar creak in the door hinges that needed oiling. The shadow was in the room! The dark shadow loomed forward, getting closer and closer to its intended target—a helpless young girl who was just coming into puberty, learning her own lithe body, still embarrassed and in awe of her budding breasts.

It, the monster, the boogeyman was at the very edge of her bed now. Ever so gently, its hands caressed the ruffled bedspread. Smoothed it back down. Because of her heightened sense of smell, the girl could smell the familiar body odor that assaulted her nostrils. The little girl's body stiffened instantly. She felt the clammy hand touch her shoulder and gently shake her awake. Even through her pj's, the new ones that her mom had recently bought her for being good, the touch disgusted her and made her recoil like a turtle into its shell.

"Hey, princess, are you asleep?" the monster whispered in a drunken, slurred speech. The words ran together.

Behind tightly closed eyes, the little girl prayed silently to God. Maybe God would hear this time. Dear God, I promise to be good, eat all my vegetables, do what Mama tells me to do, do good in school. I'm scared. Make this monster go away. MAKE IT GO AWAY!

Ten

After dropping off and unpacking the couple of bags of groceries, I was eager for a long, unhurried night of Redman. Earlier, I had reorganized the cabinets in the kitchen. For anyone who knew her, it was no secret that Miss Betty was not the neatest or the most organized person. Stuff was everywhere, with no rhyme or reason. Pots and pans were mixed in with plates; silverware was just thrown in a long drawer in no particular order. If you needed a spoon, well you had to search for one like you were going on a scavenger hunt. I could never figure out how Miss Betty knew where anything was.

I didn't have to worry about leaving Miss Betty alone for the night. She was going to be okay. One of her longtime friends from church, Miss Simmons, was visiting, and they were deep into gossip mode. I overheard them discussing some deacon who got caught with a local preacher in a compromising position. I figured once they kicked back a few beers, Miss Simmons would be there for the long haul. As I was headed out the door, Miss Simmons invited me to church the next day; I hadn't been to Macedonia Baptist Church in years. I mumbled something of a response and left as quickly as I could. I didn't want to get her started. Sunday mornings were my one day of sleeping in. God understood. He rested on Sunday after creating the world. Well, on Sundays I needed rest too. Typically, I was so hungover from Saturday night that it took most of Sunday to recover.

I admit, I loved to party and have a good time. Hell, after working hard all week, I needed to kick back on the weekends. Some Sundays, Shaneeka and I would hang out. We would go out to Greenbriar or South Dekalb Mall and grab a late lunch at Piccadilly Cafeteria. We loved their veggie specials.

I had taken a long, hot shower as soon as I put away the groceries, so I didn't feel so muggy now. I had changed into a pair of denim capri pants and a low-cut dark blue blouse that tied in the back with flowing, billowy sleeves. With my braids freshly sprayed with braid sheen and pulled back off my face and my favorite lipstick on, I was looking too cute. Before I drove off, I retrieved my black duffel bag of goodies from the trunk of my car. Placed it on the front seat with me.

Before leaving Atlanta, I had made a special trip to Inserection to be on the safe side. I didn't know what the summer held for me, but I didn't want to be without some of my essentials for the bedroom. I had carried the canvas bag to the front passenger seat and expertly inspected it to make sure everything was still intact. It was all there: my various oils, lubes, handcuffs, multiple condoms in various sizes and flavors, blindfolds, sexy movies, a paddle, my feather, and a miniwhip. I was set for a night of tricks or treats and it wasn't even Halloween.

I made my way up the steps to Redman's; the usual sounds and smells met me halfway, only magnified this time. It was a Saturday night, and everyone was in full party mode as the freaks came out to play. I had knocked on his door only twice before Redman casually swung it open with the beginnings of a high already apparent. The smell of weed greeted my nostrils as I stepped inside his apartment. Redman had on sagging blue jeans that revealed the top portion of his black underwear and a black and white Atlanta Hawks basketball jersey. His cornrows, courtesy of me, were still looking neat and shiny. He focused on me with a slight smirk on his full lips and those sexy bedroom eyes silently seduced me. Made me want to strip down butt naked then and there. However, we had all night. There wasn't a need to rush.

"What's up? What took you so long? I expected you over an hour ago," he asked, stepping back so that I could enter the living room.

"I told you I had to run to the store first," I said impatiently, innocently dropping my goodie bag on the floor by his door.

"What's in the bag? You spending the night?" he asked, reaching down to retrieve it.

I quickly shoved it to the side with my left foot. "You'll find out soon enough. Quit being so damn nosy," I teased.

"Come here, you," he said, pulling me into his solid mass and draping one hand around my shoulder while the other hand held tightly to his weed.

"You gonna be my bad girl tonight?" he teasingly asked, kissing me on the back of my neck. Instantly, I felt chill bumps run up and down my arms.

"You'll have to wait and see. Won't you?"

As he licked his full lips, he looked me up and down. "Yeah, I'll wait. Your pussy's worth waiting for.

"You want a beer?" he asked, walking into his tiny, bland kitchen and opening the refrigerator that was on its last leg.

"Yeah, bring me one. Hell, bring me two. I'm ready to let loose tonight. And pull up those damn pants. I see your drawers," I joked.

"Better yet, why don't you come over and pull them off for me?"

"Can I drink my beer in peace?" I asked, retrieving it from him and sitting down on the sofa.

"Okay. Okay, that's cool for now. So what's up with you and Miss Betty?"

"The usual petty bullshit. That woman gets on my last damn nerve, but I'm not here to talk about her. Not tonight anyway. I have other plans that involve you and me and body parts."

"Do you, now?"

"You better believe it."

Redman reclined back and stared at me with admiring, droopy eyes.

"What?"

"You something else. I don't meet many women like you. The kind not into playing head games and shit. And you don't try to ration your pussy like it's some precious gem to get you what you want."

"Why should I? I like to fuck as much as you. You got something I need too."

"And what's that?" he asked with a knowing smirk.

"It's between your legs."

I made myself at home, kicked off my sandals and took a big puff on the blunt Redman had left in the ashtray on the coffee table. Immediately, I felt myself start to unwind and get an "I don't care attitude" as I laid my head back on the sofa and stared over at the TV in the corner.

I picked up Redman's remote control and unmuted the volume. Redman had some porno movie going full force. The typical big-breasted, big-butt woman was giving some man the best head of his life as corny music played in the background. Where did they get that music? From the intense facial expressions and the savage moans he was making, the Jamaican-looking guy with the humongous dick and long dreadlocks wasn't going to last much longer before he exploded all over her face and mouth. I was still trying to figure out how she was putting all of him in her mouth without gagging. Better yet, how was she going to fit all of him inside her? Somebody needed to research why Jamaican men are so hung. Is it really just the climate and their diets?

Redman noticed my fascination with the images on screen.

"You like that, don't you? That shit turns you on, Mer."

"No, it doesn't. I am just checking out the rod on that guy."

"Yeah, right. Anyway, you've seen bigger."

"Where?"

"Here," he said, reaching down and stroking himself through his jeans.

"Yeah, in your dreams." I laughed.

"You know how to stroke a man's ego, don't you?" he said, strutting back into the kitchen. The munchies were in full effect.

"Oh, did I hurt your feelings, boo?"

"Hell no. I know what I'm working with."

"It's all good. Because believe me, if you had all that, you most definitely wouldn't be getting up in my stuff."

"Is that right?"

"Yeah, man. You best believe it."

"Well, tell me what can I do for you tonight?" Redman asked as he reentered the room with another cold beer, chips and a big all-knowing grin on his face. I couldn't help it. That brought a tiny smile to my face, and for the moment I forgot about my issues with Miss Betty.

Eleven

With Redman, I felt like I was home; it was always that way with us. I didn't have to act like somebody I wasn't. Like I had to do at the bank day in and day out. With him I didn't have to pretend; I could let my guard down and just be myself. I could say whatever the hell I felt like saying. Redman didn't judge me. Never had. And there was something about thuggish men that turned me on. I still had dreams of getting with the rapper 50 Cent, only for one night. I bet 50 could throw down. That entire bad-boy, macho persona did it every time. Redman knew what I liked. He knew that a little aggression during sex heightened the passion level. An ounce of pain made it all the more delicious, and he indulged me because we were two of a kind. Two peas in a fucking pod.

"I don't know what you can do for me. You tell me."

"What's up?"

Redman plopped down on his sagging sofa a few inches from me, leaned over and gave me an all-knowing look as his warm tongue found mine. He tongued me down thug style and squeezed my breasts a little too hard at the same time. I moaned softly. Immediately I felt myself get hot, and a wetness crept forth inside my bikini panties.

Redman stopped his assault on my mouth long enough to

unzip his jeans, pull his large dick out with his legs gaped wide open. "Why don't you come over here and hook me up like the bitch in the movie?"

"Bitch?"

"That's right, like that bitch. Don't trip, Mercedes. I didn't call you one. I said like the one in the movie."

"Whatever. And why don't you come over here and do what you do best, baby?"

"What? You want me to eat your pretty pussy, baby?" he asked, placing his large hand between my legs and starting to gently rub. "That shit turns you on, don't it? You be about to lose your mind."

I shook my head and opened my legs wider as his finger found my spot. In my mind, I could already picture us getting busy.

"Don't get all shy and quiet on me now. Tell me. Let me hear you say what you want, what you need," he demanded, simultaneously unbuttoning my pants and pulling them down to my ankles, along with my panties, so that he could have better access to place his fingers inside me.

Two fingers slowly worked their way in, my body involuntarily jerked slightly, my breathing sped up and Redman expertly made up and down movements within me.

"I ain't telling you shit," I said in a husky, joking manner.

"No? You'll tell me. You want me to do you too bad." He laughed, inserting yet another finger inside me and slowly moving them around, in and out. All the way in and almost out, teasing me ever so slowly as his other hand roamed and massaged my 36C breasts. My wetness seeped onto his fingers.

"Say it. Your sexy voice turns me on. Makes my dick hard as steel."

"No. You know what to do. I ain't begging for shit," I said half-heartedly, closing my eyes as I bit on my lower lip.

By now, Redman had my blouse off and had eased me down

onto the sofa and was working me over. My loud moans are louder than the lady on the porno movie who was now being sexed by the Jamaican man and his muscular friend. They were definitely having their way with her.

"You feel too good baby. So hot and wet, burning up. I'm waiting to hear you tell me. You ain't getting shit until you ask for it, beg for it," he whispered near my ear, bending down and teasingly flicking his tongue down to my nipples. My body tingled. I shook my head. I closed my eyes tighter and clenched my teeth because I didn't want him to hear my moans and see the effect that just his fingers and mouth were having on me.

Suddenly he stopped. Stopped touching me. Stopped the good feeling. Redman sat up and took another drag on the blunt and looked at me from behind half-closed eyes, waiting. Waiting like he had all the time in the world. By now the woman in the video was being fulfilled orally. One brother had her legs wide open while the other one had fingers and his mouth tearing her stuff up.

"Okay, you win," I cried out, having an overwhelming need to be satisfied.

Redman eased another finger into my slippery wetness and started his rhythm again. I rose up to meet him halfway.

"I'm waiting. Tell me what you want."

"I want you to eat me," I whispered.

"What? I can't hear you? Say it louder," he whispered, pulling his fingers out and a playful smile appearing on his face.

"Eat me," I requested a little louder.

"What? Say that again?"

"Eat my pussy!"

Redman could hear the urgency in my voice and feel my body tremble for him like an addict looking for a crack fix. He was enjoying this too damn much.

"Well, maybe if you're a good girl and do what I tell you, I'll give you what you want. Come here," he said, roughly pulling me up by my shoulders.

In my nakedness, I scooted over closer to him and looked up at him expectantly.

Redman was playing with me and obtaining too much joy from it. He spread my legs as wide as he could and started to play there some more. My moans blended in with the woman in the movie who now had one man giving her head and the Jamaican god stroking and sucking her breasts.

"No, baby, come down here. Get on your knees between my legs."

"Why?"

"Just do what I say. Trust me."

I hesitantly scooted onto the floor and did as he said. He rubbed his hands across my face with such tenderness.

"I intend to make you so hot that you beg me to screw you." Suddenly he jerked my chin up and made me look at him. We were face-to-face. All we could hear were the sex sounds emitted from the movie and my rapid breathing. He kissed me again, roughly. I tried to pull away. Redman pulled me back into him and started to tweak my nipples again, a little too furiously.

"Stop it!" That shit was hurting now. I attempted to pull away.

"Oh, you don't like that? Get your ass back here." Pulling me back, Redman immediately started to tweak my nipples between his fingers again. My nipples were throbbing, but responding through the pain.

"I know you, Mercedes. You like it rough. The rougher it is, the harder you come. My little freak," he laughed as he kissed me on the forehead.

"Now, give Lester some love." Lester is what he called his dick. Redman pulled my head down.

"No, boo, not yet. Do me first."

"Suck this big black dick, girl. It's in need of a warm space," he said, grabbing a handful of my braids and shoving my head down.

"Leave me alone." Redman didn't release his strong hold.

"Baby, you know you like this," he said, rubbing Lester across my face and down to my mouth. He smacked my backside with his open hand. As pain exploded across my ass, I winced.

I slowly but hesitantly opened my mouth. He let out a loud moan as Lester went in. His hands guided my head up and down. Up and down, ever so slowly. Then faster. His legs opened wider. I took in more. Up and down. Up and down.

"Good girl. Yeah, good girl. Now lick under my balls. Yeah, that's good. Shit that's good."

He still had his hands entwined in my braids, and when I hesitated, the pulling pressure increased. I licked and sucked, he moaned and groaned, and just like in the movie, I looked up just as his eyes started to roll back in his head. When Redman finished enjoying the moment, he wasted no time; he shoved the coffee table out of the way and expertly pushed me down and placed me upon the worn gray carpet.

For the next thirty minutes, he gave me what I desired. Redman had a magic tongue. I lost count of how many times I came. Whenever it was too delicious, I tried to pull away, but he never let up on his tight grasp on my thighs. He proceeded to handle my stuff.

However, we are not done yet. The night was still young as we tested different oils from my bag. At one point, Redman had me on the floor on all fours while he banged me aggressively from behind. He was ramming me so hard that I was inching across the carpet getting carpet burns on my tender knees. After a while I couldn't distinguish between the pain or the pleasure. It all meshed into one delicious feeling that was even more pronounced with my high.

"Lester's making that pussy feel good, ain't he?"

When I wouldn't answer, he'd smack me on the ass with his open palm.

"Talk to me! Answer me dammit!" *Whack! Whack!*

I didn't respond. He spanked my ass again and again as he thrust deeper inside me. A tingling, burning sensation coupled with his thrusts greeted my throbbing body. I felt like every pore on my body was exposed, like I was an open wound. I felt.

"Yes, spank that ass! Show me who's the man! Oh, it feels good! Faster! Faster, damn it!" I screamed as my intense feeling lifted me to a higher plateau. I floated up, up and away, and poof, all my problems evaporated.

"That's right, tell me to spank that ass again."

"No," I said, bracing in anticipation of his hand coming down on my butt cheek yet again.

"Tell me, goddammnit!"

"No," I screamed, tears stinging my eyes.

He slapped and rubbed my ass again as his hand encircled my neck.

"I'm going to spank your ass again and again until you learn to do what I say. This belongs to me, and don't you ever forget it," he declared between thrusts.

By now, I was delirious as my moans blended in with those in the movie. Redman pulled out.

"Are you going to be a good girl?" he asked, fondling my breasts and playing with my nipples.

I was almost about to cry, I wanted him back in me so bad. "Yes, baby, yes. Please put Lester back in."

Instead of obliging my requests, he pushed me down onto my

back and lifted my legs onto his shoulders as his tongue, once again, found my spot. The magic tongue. Instant waves of spasms exploded throughout my body. Suddenly, I felt an unbelievably intense feeling as fireworks exploded and it was like the Fourth of July in the projects.

"Yeah, that's my good girl."

However, Redman wasn't finished. After I had calmed down, he pulled me upright.

"Open your mouth," he demanded. "I got something for you," he said, his fingers massaging my spot.

I did as he asked and the rain came down in hot spurts.

"Good girl."

Around two a.m., after another restless sleep in which I tossed and turned, I untangled myself from Redman's embrace and redressed. My ass was still throbbing from where his dark hand lashed out punishment.

I'd spent the last fifteen minutes staring at a medium-sized roach crawl from one end of the wall to another. The roach finally found a home behind a framed picture of the silhouette of a nude black woman hanging on his wall. I knew where there was one roach, there were many others.

I looked down at him as he slept. Redman was out for the count. I knew it would probably be weeks before I saw him again. Not wanting to wake him, I made sure I had my car keys in hand as I quietly let myself out. I drove home sore, but fully satisfied.

"Come on, princess, I know you aren't sleep. You just playing possum," the monster said, swiftly tossing Sweetmouth to the side of the bed and out of the way. The girl wanted to reach out and save Sweetmouth from the space between the bed and the wall, or maybe it was the other way around. She wanted Sweetmouth to save her.

"I know you aren't sleep. Wake up, princess. It's time to play our secret game again. Remember, this is our special game that's just between you and me," the monster said, pulling and tugging her new pj's down to her knees.

The little girl closed her eyes as tightly as she could. So tight that she saw swirling white specks that danced around in playful circles. Involuntarily, she reached out her right hand to try and join the dancing specks. They were having so much fun. Dancing around in amazing circles. Small circles, then big ones. The white specks and other vibrant colors thrown in the mix. As the girl went to that other place she sometimes visited, the dark, safe place, the assault began on her tiny, helpless body.

Before she entirely surrendered to the other place, she heard the monster say, "Be a good girl now, princess. You know you like it."

Twelve

Sunday morning had me unexpectantly taking Miss Simmons up on her offer. I didn't know what got into me. I surprised myself by getting up early and preparing eggs, grits, bacon and orange juice for Miss Betty and myself. And then I happily dressed for morning church service, which began promptly at eleven o'clock.

Miss Betty and I had quietly and silently come to an unspoken truce. She didn't ask me about my whereabouts the previous night or even mention our argument. Thank goodness.

We actually had a civil breakfast. Miss Betty caught me up on some juicy gossip regarding various people in the neighborhood. I knew that's what her and Miss Simmons were so animated about in their conversation the night before. After breakfast, I dressed in a simple multicolored sundress with slip-on mules. I hadn't brought too many dresses from home, other than my work attire, because I hadn't planned on attending church service anywhere. Today I didn't feel like wearing one of my stuffy business suits.

I drove over to Macedonia Baptist Church, which was about twenty minutes from the house, and I thought back to the previous night. I didn't feel ashamed anymore. I realized there were many others like me. I had done Internet research on this topic; I was not alone in my desires. At first I had thought I was just a freak.

I didn't know when or how I started liking rough sex. It kind of slipped up on me without me realizing it was something I desired. Now I craved it. It made me feel alive. Redman dug it as well. Well, actually, Redman just dug sex any way he could get it. Don't get me wrong. I didn't have sex like that all the time, maybe fifty percent of the time. The other fifty percent of the time, I was just as normal as everybody else.

A lot of times, the men I slept with were not down with hitting, dominating or knocking a woman around. In time, I learned to provoke some of them into it by name-calling, picking fights, etc. I'd get them so mad that they'd go off without even realizing it, and somehow we'd end up in bed, making up.

Looking back, I think that's how it all started with me. Back in high school, in the ninth grade, maybe tenth, I had this crazy-ass boyfriend. I was crazy about him, had my nose wide open. I thought I loved him. That's funny now. I would have done anything for him. Anything. However, I later learned the fool enjoyed roughing up women. He got off on the thrill of inflicting pain or maybe the adrenaline of dominating another person with no shame.

He had a reputation for having a quick temper and had gotten suspended many times for fighting, but he always treated me with respect. At first I thought it was cute how he'd get jealous over some guy he thought I liked or had looked at. Thought it proved he loved me. Yet he had never hit me. Shook me, pushed me, but never hit me. When we screwed, it was so-so. Nothing to write home about. It was still that clumsy, teenage sex. And hell, I was just going through the motions; I didn't know what to do either.

Anyway, to make a long story short, the fool, Clifton—yeah that's his name—got mad at me one night at the skating rink. Back in the day, everyone used to hang out at the skating rink on Sunday nights, on Soul Night. Soul Night was nothing short of a big party. People didn't come to really skate. Everyone came to be seen, get phone numbers, and parade the latest fashions. I don't know why the black folk always got Sunday night as party night.

Anyhow, I'll never forget that night; it was a humid summer night, and Clifton beat the shit out of me in the parking lot of the skating rink, in the backseat of his red hooptie car. He had this crazy notion that I had given my phone number to some guy from our rival basketball team. I know, now it sounds silly. However, at the time it wasn't funny. After tricking me to his car and promptly beating my ass, he wanted to fuck me.

Clifton apologized over and over and actually started crying. Rubbed my face with the side of his hand and told me, again and again, how sorry he was that he hurt me. And there I sat with a black eye, busted lip, torn shirt and a jacked-up new skirt. So much for a fashion statement.

Clifton apologized over and over again some more and then started to touch me. I felt his hand as it made its way under my short skirt. I was repulsed. I hit at his hands, kicked and tried with all my might to get him away, off me. The harder I tried to get him off me, the more determined he became to feel me up. I saw that look cross his face again, that "I'm going to jack you up" look. I guess Clifton felt I was rejecting him again.

My fear excited him. My ghetto survival instinct kicked in, and I let him do what he wanted to do, and since he still had some of that pent-up anger left, he wasn't gentle.

At first I felt humiliated; then I couldn't pretend any longer; my body betrayed me, and it was feeling too good as he finger fucked me and later sexed me as he made me ride him. That was the best sex we ever had.

I felt strange. I can't explain it, but I felt high to know that a man loved me enough to beat my butt because he thought I was creeping on him. It was also the last time I saw him after Miss Betty forced me, after seeing my face, to tell her what he had done to me. Shortly afterwards, Clifton went to live with relatives up North with the threat of a severe ass beating following close behind him. I never saw him again, yet I never forgot that feeling. For a moment in time, I felt.

Thirteen

I finally pulled up into the church's parking lot; I was lucky to find an empty parking space. Since I was running about fifteen minutes late, the service had already begun. This particular church didn't run on colored-people time. As I was walking up the narrow walkway and saw other churchgoers arriving, I was relieved that I wasn't the only late person. I remembered that as a child I used to love to come to this church with my grandmother. Miss Betty wasn't what you would call a religious person. After growing up in a strict, religious household, I think she rebelled once she got out from under her mother's strict roof.

In fact, today some would say that I wasn't brought up in a good Christian environment with Miss Betty. Today, under the same circumstances, the Department of Family and Children's Services would probably take me away and place me in foster care. I admit I saw a lot as a child. I knew a lot of things the average child didn't and shouldn't have known. Macedonia Baptist Church was like a safe house or haven; I always felt the warmth the minute I walked through the doors. It was like an invisible arm embraced and protected me.

This morning was no different. I embraced the sense of family, community, history and unity the minute I stepped over the threshold. I secured a program from the friendly male usher at the

door and was directed to a seat near a front pew. Of course. When
you are late, you are always paraded to the front of the church. I
felt all eyes were on me as I shyly sat down. I quietly greeted the
women sitting to my left and right as I lowered my head to read
the program. I'd only missed devotional service. Good.

The service was uplifting. I sensed my spirits rise, which I
needed because Monday was the start of another week at work
with those idiots. I needed as much inspiration as I could receive.
The choir was off the chain, and I realized how much I missed
and needed this back in Decatur. There were many large churches
in the metro Atlanta area, like New Birth, but I made no efforts
to attend. The service went by quickly as the robust pastor
preached a powerful, stimulating sermon that had everyone on
his or her feet clapping and praising the Lord as they shouted
"Amen. Hallelujah."

Yet throughout the entire service, I couldn't get over the uneasy
feeling that somebody was staring at me. Watching me. When I'd
glance around discreetly, I didn't see anyone. Everyone was into the
pastor and his message of hope for the state of the nation. There
were several families who had sons or daughters fighting in the
war. There was one family that had both a father and mother of
two children serving. In the meantime, the two daughters, ages
four and six years old, were living with their maternal grandmother. Everyone was asked to keep them in their prayers. Many
people had lost jobs due to downsizing or layoffs. One slim, attractive sister testified how she lost her job of ten years recently. Calls
for prayer were going out to all. President Bush was going to pay
for this in the next election.

When the program came to a conclusion, the pastor asked
everyone to greet and hug his or her neighbors. Tell them you
loved them. I hesitantly hugged a few people I didn't know from

Adam or Eve when a strong arm embraced me from behind and said, "Imagine this, the woman of few words. Good to see you."

I turned around and looked up into the admiring eyes of Darius, the guy from Piggly Wiggly.

"Darius?" I asked, pulling away from his strong embrace.

"I see you remember my name. That's a good sign," he said, a smile lighting up his entire face and that dimple standing out like a marquee sign.

"You're looking gorgeous today. Did you enjoy the service?" he asked, gently pulling me out of the path of churchgoers exiting the church.

"Huh? Yeah. Are you following me or something?" I asked in honest disbelief.

"Mercedes, I'm a member of this church, joined a few months ago. I felt it was time to work on my spirituality. Believe me. I'm not a deranged, stalking lunatic. You're safe with me, baby."

I smiled my first smile of the day. "That's good to know," I said, checking him out from head to toe.

He was looking too fine in that black suit, black shoes, bald head and goatee. I could just eat him up and come back for seconds with a thick slice for dessert.

"The lady can smile. And a beautiful smile it is."

"I wasn't that bad the other evening, was I?"

"Has Michael Jackson turned into a white woman?"

We both laughed at that one. In spite of myself, I felt myself relaxing.

"Oh, you're a comedian today, are you?" I asked, playfully touching his left arm and feeling solid mass.

"I am if I can see that beautiful smile again."

"You're too much. Are you always so complimentary of the ladies?"

"Only you, baby. I told you, you do something to me."

"What do I do to you? Break it down for me."

"If only you knew."

"Educate me. I'm listening."

"I couldn't even begin to explain the ways here. It would take too long and would give these nosy mothers something to talk about into next week. I'd love to tell you over dinner how you make me weak in my knees."

"Dinner? Oh, I don't . . ."

"Mercedes, stop," he said, holding up his right hand. "As much as I'm attracted to you, I'm not going to beg you like some little schoolboy to go out to dinner with me."

"What? Excuse me?" I couldn't believe what he had just said to me.

"That's right. You heard me right. I'm sure you have men chasing after you left and right, lined up, but baby I don't have to beg. I know I'm a good, decent man. And if you can't see that, well, your loss."

"Is that right?" I asked in a playful, sexy tone.

"Damn right!" he laughed, instantly lowering his voice in the house of the Lord.

"Well, I guess I'll have to take you up on your offer to find out for myself if you're all that, a bag of chips and a dill pickle."

"Just say the word and it's done. When and where? And I'll deliver."

"Can you really deliver? I'm pretty hard to please."

"Yeah, I can deliver one hundred percent to your satisfaction. I promise," he whispered into my ear, letting me know he had picked up on my innuendo.

"You sure about that? You wouldn't be wasting my time? My time is too valuable and precious."

"Don't worry your pretty head about that. See, your problem is that you haven't met a real man yet. My actions speak for me. Actions speak louder than words."

"Okay, meet me at Applebee's, the one on Main Street. Friday at eight o'clock."

"I can pick you up. Give me your address."

"No, I'd rather meet you."

"Mercedes, you don't have to run from me. But I will do what the lady wishes. Well, listen, I have to run. But you have a great day, Miss Mercedes."

"You too, Mr. Darius."

"I'll be counting the days to Friday."

"You do that."

"Five days to go and counting," he said, confidently walking off.

As he walked off, my thoughts of me and him dancing between the sheets were interrupted when Miss Simmons, dressed in a suit and hat, tapped me on my shoulder and pulled me into yet another embrace. "I thought that was you. Good to see you, baby."

Later that day, Miss Betty asked me who was the attractive man I was talking to in church. She even described him to a tee, dimple and all. It didn't come as a surprise to me that the gossip grapevine was alive and well. I just didn't know they worked so fast. I couldn't help but laugh. I told Miss Betty I didn't know yet, but I was going to try my best to find out.

Miss Betty was like, "What in the hell is that suppose to mean?" She shook her head and rolled her wheelchair back into her bedroom for a nap.

"I'll let you know," I shouted to her.

"Mer, stop talking in riddles. Maybe this is a good thing. Maybe you need a good, decent church boy to slow you down," she called out from her bedroom.

"I doubt it," I murmured under my breath. "I could probably show him some thangs. I could throw a little something on him and turn him out. Have him feenin for me."

"Wake me up in a hour."

"Okay." In my mind, I was thinking of letting her sleep for two. That would keep her out of my business even longer.

When the monster moved between the little girl's open legs, the child thought of happy times. She thought about trips to the Atlanta Zoo when they had extra money to spend on such things. The baby chimps were cute, the elephants looked lazy covered in mud and the giant roaches were simply gross. She thought about how her mama said she would buy her a new Barbie with some of her income-tax return money. Maybe she could get an outfit too. When would she finally get that money? The young child couldn't get her mind to remember no matter how hard she tried.

The girl thought of how much her grandmother loved her. She was sure of that. The little girl missed her so much. Big Mama would sneak her chocolate candy bars when her mama said she couldn't have any more. It was their secret. However, Big Mama died last year.

The monster's tongue was everywhere down there. The monster's long tongue made slurping sounds as it left wet trails from her budding breasts to her private area. When she felt its finger between her legs, she wanted to cry. However, she had been warned many times about crying. The monster had told her many times that no one would hear her cries. Not even her mother.

The monster stopped momentarily and looked up at the closed door. Listening. Did the monster hear something? Was someone coming to rescue the little girl? No such luck. The monster quickly went back to touching itself and the little girl down there. The monster's breathing changed, was coming quickly now. There was a slight tremble.

It was over. Then the monster straightened back up and proceeded to hastily redress the girl. All the while, it whispered in her ear, "Remember, this is our little secret. This is how I show you I love you. I love you, princess."

The girl didn't hear much of what was said. She had heard it too many times before. The girl was just glad it was over for now. Again she had survived it. And again no one had rescued her. Not even her mama.

Fourteen

Believe it or not, I was somewhat nervous about meeting Darius at Applebee's; the restaurant was a common Friday-night hangout for singles. I hadn't quite figured out why I was anxious. There was something about him that I couldn't put my finger on yet.

The week at work went by quickly enough. Thank goodness. It was already becoming the same ol', same ol'. I had pretty much set the women at the banking center straight, professionally of course; they now knew how to step to me. I realized my job wasn't major to a lot of people; I recognized I wasn't a vice president; just give me a few years though. Nevertheless, I was proud at how far I had come.

Most girls I went to school with ended up pregnant before eleventh grade; some didn't even graduate. They were lucky if they received their GEDs. The majority of them didn't attend college, go to the military or do anything significant with their lives. They got caught up in generational poverty and never bettered themselves. Now they were still living in the projects, thirty years old, looking forty-five. Sad. You could drive over to the projects I grew up in and see mothers, aunts and their daughters all living in the same projects. No one gets out. Living off the state. Sad. I was determined that that wasn't going to be me. That wasn't going to be my life.

After work, I promptly rushed home to prepare a light meal of spaghetti and a garden salad for Miss Betty and to get ready for my meeting, date, whatever you wanted to call it, with Darius. During the week, I had told Shaneeka all about him when we chatted on the phone. Even though my girl was a little down in the dumps thanks to Jamal, she was more excited about my date than I was. I had to promise to call her the very next day with all the details. She wanted me to call her that night, but I refused.

I had thought long and hard about it and realized that Darius could be good company for me during the summer. He looked like he had some serious skills with those big-ass feet. The feet and hands on a man told their own story. Darius certainly had a knack with words and that dimple was irresistible.

I finally decided on jeans and a simple blue halter top that showed my full and ample chest. I wanted to tease him a bit tonight. See where his mind was. Darius could look, but not touch. Those were my rules. Who knows? Maybe he'd get lucky, and I'd let him cop a feel or two. Then again, maybe not. I was running this show. I intentionally arrived a few minutes late for our date. It was always good to make them wait on you, train them from the get-go. I didn't want to show up early and appear too anxious.

I pulled up into the overcrowded parking lot and had to park all the way in the very back and walk up to the front. The place was already populated with patrons enjoying a lovely, star-filled Friday night out on the town. I had totally forgotten that this was small-town America with only a few restaurants to choose from. It appeared that everyone had chosen this restaurant tonight. I walked in and was straining my neck to look around. I didn't see Darius anywhere. Maybe he was late; if so, I was out the door. If I didn't see him in five minutes, I was history. I refused to wait on a man.

When I felt strong, solid arms embrace my waist from behind,

I slowly turned around. "There you are. You were making me nervous. Thought you had stood me up."

"Now what would have given you that idea?" I asked, innocently staring up into his handsome face. Darius was looking and smelling wonderful. He had decided on black jeans and a pullover polo-style shirt. It was simple, but defined all the right muscles in his arms and chest.

Darius just smiled down at me like he was happy to see me. He wasn't too tall or too short. And I loved the natural curl of his dark eyelashes.

"I've already put us on the waiting list. So it shouldn't be much longer on a table. Maybe another fifteen minutes," he said, guiding me by the arm to a far corner wall so that we'd be out of the way of the constantly opening front door.

"That's cool."

It was so crowded in the place that we were involuntarily hugged up in the corner like a couple in love. "So how was your week?"

"Okay. Work is work. You know. Same ol', same ol'."

"True, I hear that. Well, I thought about you. It helped the week go by quickly. I kept thinking about seeing your lovely face today when I was driving and delivering packages all over town."

"Cool."

"Cool?" He laughed. "Is that all you can say?"

"What do you want me to say?"

"I don't know. Maybe I thought about you too."

"What if I didn't?"

He just chuckled. "You are too much girl."

"No, just honest."

"Well, you just give me some time. I'm gonna have you thinking about me day and night. You'll see."

"You think so?"

"I know so, 'cause I got it like that. You gonna be blowing up my pager, cell and home phone."

"Yeah right. Don't hold your breath."

"Oh, you wrong for that, Mercedes."

Finally our table was ready. The perky hostess led us to a booth in the nonsmoking section, and we were seated. I was kind of disappointed because I was digging our closeness. The way his body felt pressed up against mine was sexy. My body meshed into his perfectly.

After we were comfortably seated across from each other in a secluded booth near the back of the restaurant and had studied the menu, there was an awkward silence for a few seconds. Darius leaned back and took me in with his eyes. Suddenly I felt self-conscious. Like I needed to cover up or something.

"You're wearing that top, Miss M?"

"Oh, you noticed, huh?"

"Yeah, I couldn't help but notice. I'd have to be Stevie Wonder not to. You putting all the other women in here to shame."

Secretly, I smiled, because I knew that my best features were my breasts and butt, and believe me, I played them up whenever I could. Like that song from back in the day, men love a big butt and a smile.

"So, Miss Mercedes, tell me about yourself."

"Like what?"

"Like where are you from? Why you moved here? The usual icebreaker-type crap that we are suppose to make on a first date. Let's get that over with now."

I smiled and thought a minute about what he asked.

"Okay, there's not much to tell. Here's the condensed version. I hope I don't bore you. I'm originally from here. I attended college

at Albany State University, moved to Decatur shortly after gradu-
ation and received a job offer at the bank. I'm temporarily here for
the summer, taking care of my mom after her knee surgery. End of
story."

"For some reason, I feel there's much more to you than that.
You come across as much more complex. More intense."

"Do I? Well, I guess you'll have to wait and see. A lady never
tells her secrets."

"Well, I guess I will. When you put it that way, you give me no
choice. Wait. Hold up. You mean I'm only going to have you for
the summer?"

"Yeah, if I let you have me. If you pass my simple tests."

"Mercedes, haven't you figured out yet that I'm irresistible?"

"I guess not," I said, a tiny smile forming on my lips.

"Ouch," was all he said, giving me that look again. That look
sent shivers up and down my spine. Luckily, I was saved by the
waitress as she came to take our drink orders.

Fifteen

In the midst of a noisy, half-drunken, crowded restaurant on a Friday night, I learned all about Darius. As we ate our appetizers of buffalo wings with celery and blue cheese dressing, drank several strawberry daiquiris and ate our entrees, I was introduced to his world. Darius, thirty-four, worked for UPS, was newly divorced and was struggling to put his life back together. He'd left and divorced his wife, Latrice, a little over a year ago, after she got strung out on crack. When he was talking about his ex it was the only time during the evening that his mood wasn't upbeat. Other than that, he was an average, hard-working Joe Blow. End of his story.

To my surprise, the night came to an end all too soon. As we were waiting for our waitress to bring over the check, Darius asked me the question I couldn't escape.

"Why haven't you been snatched up and married with two kids by now?"

"You and my mama ask the same questions?"

"Seriously."

I shrugged and looked away to study the twenty-to-thirty-something crowd. "I don't know. Marriage isn't for me. I'm not looking to give up my identity to stroke some man's ego for the rest of my life. It's not me and never will be. It has always been me, myself and I."

There was a silence for a few minutes. I continued to study the crowd and wait on his response. I knew it would come with an objection to my theory.

"Interesting theory, Mercedes. Even though my marriage didn't work out, marriage is a wonderful thing when two people who love each other come together and are willing to build a life and family together. There's something fulfilling to be said for that."

"And the woman gives ninety percent while the husband gives maybe ten percent, and then five years into it, he leaves her for some younger hussy he meets in a club. No. No, thank you."

"You are a true cynic."

I shrugged again. "Whatever. I consider myself a realist."

"Whatever," he mocked, reaching across the wooden table to hold my hand. I pulled back like I'd been burned by fire. Our waitress, Amber, returned to save the day once again. Darius just glanced at me, but didn't say anything about my reactions. Amber asked if everything was okay, gave us our complimentary mints, handed the check to Darius, and glided away with a cheery, fixed smile.

"You just haven't met the right man yet."

"I guess not, or maybe I'm not looking for him."

"Maybe he'll find you. When you least expect it. Life works like that sometimes."

"I seriously doubt it."

"You never know. Life is funny like that."

"If you say so, Mr. Philosopher."

Once Darius paid the tab and left a tip, we slowly made our way out the door and into the still-crowded parking lot. Darius passed my first test with flying colors. He didn't expect me to split the check. I didn't pay for anything. Screw women's rights. I was not going dutch on any date. If a man wanted to be in my presence, well, he had to pay for it.

Cars were constantly pulling into the restaurant parking lot and there was a line of people still waiting for their tables. It was early, and I was not ready to go home.

"I'm parked over there, in the very back," I pointed. "Where are you?"

"Over there." He pointed towards the front of the building.

"How did you manage to get so close to the front?"

"I don't know about you, but my mama taught me to always be on time."

I glanced at him, but didn't comment on his sly remark.

"Come on, I'll walk you." This time, he didn't try to hold my hand. He lightly placed his arm around my shoulder as I gazed up at the night sky and enjoyed the moment.

"You don't have to walk me all the way back there."

"Well, I'm a gentlemen, or can't you tell? I wouldn't want anything to happen to you. I need you to make it home safe and sound."

"Yeah, you are pretty decent."

"Oh no, my first compliment from Mercedes. I must remember this moment in detail."

"Whatever." I smiled, touching his arm.

"And hurry up and get home before the storm catches you. Drive carefully."

I looked up at the clear, star-filled night sky. "What storm?"

"The storm that must be coming since you complimented me."

I just laughed and looked at him like he was as crazy as a loon. By now we had made it to my car.

"Well, I enjoyed myself. Thanks for dinner."

"Did you really? Enjoy yourself?"

"Yes, it was fun. I have to admit, you're pretty cool. The evening flew by."

"Well, it doesn't have to end yet," he said, looking at me anxiously. "In fact, I was hoping we could hang out awhile longer. There is still so much I don't know about you. You are one mysterious lady."

"I don't know. I really should get back to Miss Betty."

"Who?"

"Oh, that's what I call my mama. We are quite the dysfunctional family; you won't find the Huxtables at our house," I exclaimed in all seriousness. He knew I was not joking this time.

"It can't be that bad."

"No, only worse."

"Well, maybe you can tell me about it another time," he said, inching himself up into my face. I was leaning against my car door, and Darius was only inches from me. I felt nervous and silly all at the same time. Like a schoolgirl on a first date.

"Well?"

"Well what?"

"When are we doing this again? I have to get you to commit now since you won't give me your home, cell or work number."

"Next Saturday is cool. I know this jazz club that's really a hole in the wall, but the jazz is smooth."

"You like jazz?"

"I dig whatever you like."

"Cool."

"Yeah, cool."

"Well, give me your number so I can call you in the meantime. You can tell me all about your dysfunctional family and how it produced such a wonderful lady despite the drama."

"I'm not wonderful," I said a bit too harshly and swiftly.

Darius looked down at me. I looked away. I didn't want him to see my pain.

"I know what I see. You are a bit rough around the edges, but wonderful nevertheless. A diamond in the rough."

I felt shy and glanced down, once again, at my feet. No one had ever told me I was wonderful before.

"Well, am I getting the digits?"

"You know where I work. Stop by next week, and I'll give them to you then."

"Oh, you like to play games, huh?"

"No, not really. I just want to make it adventurous for you."

"Yeah, right. But you're cute. Very cute."

"So are you."

"You're at the bank over on Oak Street?"

"That's the one. Not far from the Subway on the corner."

"Don't sweat it. I'll stop by to see your pretty face. I'm not going to tell you when, though. This way, I'll keep you guessing; you'll look up and I'll be there."

"Please don't tell me you're one of those stalkers? Lurking in the bushes and shit?"

"You are a mess!"

"No, I'm not. You can't be too careful these days."

"Mercedes, I meant that in a good way. You know what? You could grow on me."

We stood face-to-face. Smiling for a few precious moments.

"Come here," he demanded, gently pulling me to him. Closer. I felt the heat.

"What?"

"You know what."

"No, I don't know what."

"There's one other awkward moment we have to get over."

Darius lowered his head, preparing to kiss me. At the last moment, I turned away. Couldn't do it. Couldn't give up that intimacy and closeness even for a second. To me, kissing was more intimate than the physical act of having sex.

Darius gently tapped my lips with his index finger. "Okay, not a problem. Not a problem at all. Remember what I told you, Mercedes. I don't beg. I place too much worth on myself. I'll see you next week, sweetheart," he said, turning and walking away. He didn't even look back.

I was left so totally stunned that I almost forgot to close my mouth and open my car door. By the time I pulled back up front, Darius was nowhere to be seen.

Sixteen

Miss Betty and I had quickly settled into our own little rhythm of coexistence. I performed my daughterly duties, and she kept her negative comments to a minimum. Her knee was healing properly, according to her doctor, and between her TV shows, cards and the host of friends that were in and out, she was okay. I could tell Miss Betty was getting a little cabin fever looking at the four walls all day, but at least she wasn't confined to a bed.

Work was work. Some days were rewarding, like Wednesday for instance. An elderly black woman came into the bank and wouldn't let anyone wait on her but me. She waited patiently for about thirty minutes. Once she was seated in the chair in front of my desk, she confided in me, with a big grin on her wrinkled face, that her granddaughter had informed her there was a black female working at the bank now. Mrs. Cox said she had to see this for herself, with her own two eyes, so she had her granddaughter bring her by. Mrs. Cox was a pleasure to talk to and work with. She reminded me of how much I missed a Big Mama in my life. By the time she left, I had opened a checking and savings account for her and a couple of certificates of deposit for her only granddaughter.

After the lunchtime rush, Thursday was extremely slow, and everyone was standing around praying for some customers to come through to hasten the hours. I was sitting at my desk out front, catching up on some e-mails and following up on documentation papers when out of the corner of my eye, I noticed a UPS man walk in, carrying an arrangement of colorful flowers. I went back to my tedious work. I didn't pay too much more attention to him; I just assumed it was one of my coworkers' birthdays or an anniversary, and the UPS man was making a special delivery. When the brother made a beeline straight for my desk, I started to take notice. He had my full attention, and when I heard that familiar, sexy voice, I just beamed and tingled all over.

"Beautiful flowers for a beautiful lady," Darius exclaimed, lowering the flowers down from his face and flashing that perfect set of white teeth. That dimple saluted me.

"Oh my, are these for me?" I asked, totally surprised. No man had ever given me flowers. I guess I didn't come across as a flowers type of lady. To my surprise, I found Darius's gesture so touching that my face was flushed.

"Of course. Who else would they be for?"

I bent to inhale the fragrant aroma of the colorful array of flowers in every hue under the rainbow from purples, to pinks, to various shades of reds, and Darius reveled in my simple delight.

"Don't forget the card. Read it."

I opened the small envelope to read the words Darius had inscribed just for me. It simply read: *Flowers to complement your beauty. Here's to an entire summer of getting to know you better, if you'll let me. Thinking of you. Darius.*"

I looked up, momentarily at a loss for words. "Thank you. These are beautiful! You've impressed me. I don't know what to say. You didn't have to do this."

"Well, first, I wasn't trying to impress you. I just wanted to brighten up your day. I know how you feel about this place. Second, I know I didn't have to. I wanted to. I wasn't sure if you liked roses or not, so I decided to play it safe and get you an assortment of flowers. Third, I came to get your phone number."

"Well, they're lovely, and you've succeeded in brightening my day. Thank you so much."

"You're welcome, Mercedes. You know, you're so lovely, and I don't think you realize that. Are we still on for Saturday?"

"Can't wait."

"Me either."

Neither one of us knew what to say next.

"Well, I'd better get back to work; I'm already behind schedule with my deliveries. Gonna be another long day. I had hoped you would have called me by now, but I'll see you Saturday. Enjoy the rest of your day," Darius said, tucking my phone number snugly in his breast pocket. "Seriously, you really like them?"

"Yes. I really like them."

"Cool."

"Bye, see you Saturday," I said, bending down again to inhale the sweet aroma of my bouquet. In all the excitement and surprise, I failed to notice the nosy eyes that were focused my way. I saw the way those heifers were checking out my man—oops, I mean Darius—as he left the banking center. He was looking fine in that brown uniform. It fit in all the right places. And that walk, Lord help me. Denzel Washington, or Denzie as I called him, look out.

Jennifer, the coworker who had secretly made fun of my name behind my back, made a beeline straight for my desk. She had a fake-ass smile plastered to her face. Her cohort, Ashley, was two steps behind her, silicon boobs bouncing. They were nearly tripping over each other in their rush to get all up into my business.

"Hi, Mercedes. What beautiful flowers."

"Yes, they are lovely." Ashley chimed in.

"What's the occasion?"

"There isn't one. Some of us have it like that," I gushed, laying it on strong and bending down to smell my flowers.

"Who was the hottie in the UPS uniform?" Ashley asked.

"Oh, just a friend," I replied nonchalantly.

Jennifer's blue eyes lit up in disbelief. "Just a friend?"

"Yeah."

"Oh, come on, we are all girls. You can tell us," Ashley chimed in.

"Ladies, as much as I'd like to continue this conversation, unfortunately I have tons of work to complete. Don't you?"

The Bobbsey Twins walked away with not much more information than they'd had when they strolled over. Nosy heifers. Trying to get all up in my Kool-Aid.

Seventeen

If I was on a natural high Thursday, by Friday I was at my lowest. Shaneeka called me at work around lunchtime, balling her eyes out. Until I could get her to calm down, I couldn't understand half of what she was saying. Between her sobs and trying to catch her breath, her words sounded like gibberish to me. I managed to take an early lunch break and slipped away to use the phone in a back office that provided a little more privacy.

By the time I called Shaneeka back, she was a little more composed. It seemed some bitch had the nerve, the audacity, to call Shaneeka at work, of all places, and informed her that she was pregnant with Jamal's baby. After comparing notes, some dates and times, Shaneeka believed her. When Shaneeka immediately confronted Jamal on his cell phone, he just denied everything and had the gall to hang up on her in midsentence.

Shaneeka kept asking over and over, "How could he do this to me, to us? I gave him my all and I get this, a damn slap in the face."

That shit broke my heart. I could almost feel her pain. One thing about me, I didn't have a lot of girlfriends. I didn't trust women, never have and never will. Talk about sneaky creatures, women are worse than men, always plotting, scheming and backstabbing. So needless to say, I didn't run with a crew of women.

Shaneeka was one of the few females that I truly called a friend.

She had proven time and time again that she was the real deal. The real deal didn't come around every day. And me, I was loyal to a fault. You mess with Shaneeka, then you're messing with me. That's how I felt about this matter. After an hour, I finally calmed my girl down and promised to see her later that night. I had a plan.

Immediately after work, after settling Miss Betty in, I hit the road, heading up Interstate 75N like a bat out of hell. I hadn't been home since I left for the summer, but I had serious business to attend to. Jamal was going to regret this shit. He was going to learn that you couldn't fuck over my girl, deny, deny, and fucking deny and think there wasn't going to be hell to pay. Hell no! There were going to be serious repercussions for his actions. My grandmama used to say all the time, "You reap what you sow." Well, it was time for Jamal to reap.

I put the pedal to the metal and made it back to my old apartment in record time. I was actually happy to see the place. I hadn't realize I missed it that much. After letting myself in, I found Shaneeka sitting on the sofa, in the dark, half whimpering, staring into space. I quietly placed my purse on the coffee table and went straight to her.

"Girl, I'm here now. Don't cry, sweetie. He's not worth it. We'll fix his ass. Okay?" I said, embracing her and rocking her back and forth like a newborn baby. Shaneeka looked horrible; she looked every bit the way she must feel. Her eyes were all puffy and red, her mascara had run and she hadn't bothered to wipe it off, so she had huge black streaks down her cheeks, and her clothes were disheveled like she had slept in them.

I'm not sure how long we remained in that position. Silent. No words necessary. There had been times in the past, when our roles were reversed, and I was the one in need of rocking like a baby. Those were my dark days. Days when I couldn't get out of bed, and I would cry all day. Days when my demons taunted me.

"Girl, I'm glad you're here. You're a true friend. Closer to me than my three sisters," Shaneeka whispered in between sobs that were finally tapering off.

"Yeah, I got your back. Always will."

"I know you think I'm acting like a fool, but I still love the man; I love him," she cried, bursting into fresh, heavy tears that streamed down her cheeks like a waterfall.

"I know, baby. I know you do."

"I can't help it."

"It's okay. Don't worry. I'll handle everything."

See, just another example that men are no good. Even though the signs were there for Shaneeka, she got caught up thinking her love would change him. Not. As long as Jamal had a dick, he wasn't going to change, because Jamal was too used to thinking with it. These stupid mofos didn't realize what gems they had until it was too late. It was definitely too late for Jamal.

When I finally got some vegetable soup and crackers into Shaneeka, she looked better physically even though her heart was broken in two. We spent the remainder of the night getting lit. Crazy wasted. I drove down to the package store and got some Barcardi and Coca-Cola. As fast as I could make them, we were downing those rum and cokes like they were spring water and we had been lost in the desert for days.

At some point, we fell asleep or passed out on the living room sofa. I was on one end and Shaneeka was balled up on the other corner. Even in her sleep, Shaneeka was whimpering and crying. For me, my nap was short-lived because recently I had been having restless nights, full of nightmares and unsettling images. I hadn't gotten a good night's sleep in a while. So around one a.m., I gently nudged Shaneeka with my right foot and told her it was time.

"Are you sure you want to do this?" I asked. This was her

chance to back down, because once we put my plan into action, there was no turning back.

"Hell yeah," she said, coming fully awake with a burst of renewed energy. Her eyes held fire.

"Well, let's do the damn thang!"

"Yeah, let's show that muthafuckin' nigga that he can't piss all over me without repercussions."

"Let's go. It's time to pay the piper!"

About thirty minutes later, Shaneeka and I were dressed from head to toe in all black. We had on black jeans, black T-shirts, black tennis shoes and black baseball caps. We slowly cruised by Jamal's drug-funded condo, and just as we thought, he wasn't home yet. Probably out clubbing. Unbeknownst to Jamal, Shaneeka had a key made to his prized condo months earlier.

After circling around twice, I parked my car about a block away, one street over. I retrieved my black gym bag, and then Shaneeka and I made the quick jog back to his home and efficiently and quietly entered Jamal's condo after putting on our black gloves. No words were spoken. We had work to do. The only sound made was me unzipping my gym bag and handing out supplies. Our weapons.

We worked quietly, quickly and professionally. Jamal's apartment was immaculate. His illegal activities gave him a tight crib. He actually had good taste. For some unknown reason, Jamal had a fetish for white. Everything in his crib was white. White carpet, white sofa, white walls, white knickknacks. Well, when he returned he would be seeing red, literally. We fucked that crib up! You reap what you sow!

Working as a team, Shaneeka and I managed to cut up his expensive white leather sofa and matching love seat with a straight-edged razor. Red spray paint was all over the plush carpet and pristine walls; we'd gotten creative and had all kinds of designs and patterns competing against each other. Shaneeka in her fury broke every damn picture frame that bore photos of him and her. We dumped food out of the refrigerator and the trash can into the middle of the living room floor. Chinese takeout was all over the walls. Lo mein slowly eased its way down the walls near the kitchen area like a trail of snakes.

Shaneeka and I spray painted his expensive prints hanging on the walls, cut up his king-size bed upstairs and shredded his silk sheets and comforter. We threw rolls of toilet paper in the commodes to overflow all three of his bathroom toilets. We even shattered his vanity mirrors in the bathrooms as well. Totally fucked up his place.

We stood in the foyer, which had a polished wood floor, now smelling like piss after Shaneeka relieved herself. As sweat dripped down our brows and our breathing calmed down, we high-fived each other. When we slipped out the ornate and decorative, white front door, we left one more cryptic message in red: *DON'T FUCK WITH ME, NIGGA, OR YOU'LL GET FUCKED! SORRY ASS BITCH!*

Just as quietly and swiftly as we had entered, we made our way back to my car in the cover of the starless night and sped off. On the drive home, not much was said. Ironically, V-103 was playing slow jams declaring love and devotion. We turned that shit off! After dumping any evidence of our bad deed in a large garbage can behind a convenience store, we made it safely back to the apartment. On the drive home, Shaneeka was slumped over by the passenger window, being too damn quiet. I thought she was having regrets.

Motioning wildly with her hands, she screamed, "Pull over. Pull over, Mer."

Before I could get the car over to the curb, Shaneeka had swung open the car door and was down on her hands and knees, puking in the grass. She looked a complete mess when she finally crawled back into the car and closed the door. That girl could never hold her liquor.

Before I pulled off, I reached into the dashboard and handed her some tissues.

"Are you okay, girl?"

"Yeah, I'm cool."

"You're gonna be all right."

"It doesn't feel like it."

"Time, boo. It's gonna take time."

"You tried to warn me. I was such an idiot thinking we had a future. Thinking I could change that fool."

Now wasn't the time to say I told you so. So I remained silent. I let her vent.

"Why, Mer? Why? I treated him like a king. I would have done anything for him. Why couldn't he have treated me like his queen?"

"Sweetie, I don't know why. I promise you, you'll find someone who'll treat you the way you deserve to be treated. Like a queen."

"You think so?"

"I know so. You deserve it."

"Thanks, Mer. Girl, I love you."

"I love you to, girl."

"I know you do."

By the time we made it back to the apartment, I tried to get a few hours of sleep in my room. Shaneeka had kept her promise. Everything was in place the way I left it. However, sleep wasn't forthcoming. Finally, after an hour, I gave up on finding it. I took a quick shower and changed into a short set and prepared for my long drive back. After walking around the apartment and realizing how much I missed it, I peeked in on Shaneeka.

Shaneeka was knocked out for the count, all tangled up in her sheets with her arms and legs thrown every which way. Shaneeka had always slept kind of wild. When we were children and I'd spend the night at her place, I'd usually end up on the floor with a blanket and pillow before the night was over because I couldn't stand her elbows and knees jabbing me. Looking at her, I knew she'd get past this and she'd be all right.

I left her a quick note on the kitchen table telling her to lay low, maybe even stay at her aunt's house for the rest of the weekend. And I stressed and stressed again that she was not to admit to anything. Deny, deny, deny. If push came to shove, she was to obtain a restraining order to keep Jamal away, because sooner or later he would come. Or better yet, she should get her ex-con brother to teach him another lesson. Payback is a bitch.

Eighteen

By six thirty, I was back on the highway, finishing off a breakfast of McDonald's eggs, bacon and black coffee. Man, I felt so tired. I was thirty years old, but I felt like ninety. I think, secretly, I wished for someone to show me that love was real and sacred and obtainable. But my whole life, all I'd witnessed were betrayals and hurt and pain. Like tonight.

If I was honest with myself, I envied Shaneeka because even in her pain, she felt. I had never loved anyone with that much passion, any passion. In my lifetime, I'd never loved. I'd never given anyone the permission to bring me happiness. I always knew that the only person I could depend on for my happiness was me. And lately, that was becoming more and more of an unobtainable goal. Maybe if someone bottled happiness and sold it in stores, then I could buy some. Hell, I'd purchase it by the case. That'd be a trip. Walk into Rich's-macy's and ask the salesperson for a bottle of happiness and she'd point you over to the next counter with a huge smile on her face. Even Kmart would probably have a generic version.

For a while, I drove in silence. Just thinking. Thinking of my life and what I truly wanted out of it. Before I left Miss Betty, she and I had had words. She didn't see the point in me driving all the way to Decatur to console Shaneeka; I told her I knew she wouldn't. She never saw the point.

Emotions were kept bottled up in our house when I was growing up. The more I thought back, the more I tried to pinpoint the exact date that Miss Betty started hating me. Hating her own daughter. And even more so, I tried to pinpoint the exact date that I accepted it. I was so tired. That was my reality.

I had driven for about an hour when I retrieved my cell phone from the front flap of my purse. I knew I had about 120 minutes left of prepaid minutes. I had dialed Redman's number and it had actually rung once before I pushed the End button. For some unknown reason, I didn't want to speak to him, not today anyway. I retrieved my phone book while trying not to run off the road, and found Darius's phone number scribbled in my infamous, messy handwriting. He had given me his home number again after I lied and told him that I'd lost the first one.

I was hesitant at first. Nervous. It was only a little after seven. Was it too early to call? I slowly dialed his number and pushed Send. The phone rang once, twice, three times. On the fourth ring, I was getting ready to hang up when a sleepy voice answered.

"Hello?"

"Uh, hello, Darius."

"Hello. Who is this? Mercedes?"

"Yeah, is this too early? I can call back."

"No, wait. What's up?"

"Nothing, I just thought I'd call. You say I never call."

"Baby, it's not even seven thirty on a Saturday morning. Something's got to be up."

"No, not really."

"You sure?"

"I don't know. I needed to hear—I, uh, wanted to thank you for the flowers."

"Well, as I told you before, you are very welcome. A lovely lady deserves flowers every now and then to remind her how special she is."

"Darius, you are too good to be true. You know that? You're different."

"Am I?"

"From my experiences."

"Well, you haven't been searching in the right places."

"I haven't been searching."

"Well, trust me, there are many of us out there . . . good men. Regardless of what you see on the news every night or what your girlfriends tell you, we aren't a myth that somebody made up. We are living, breathing creatures."

"I hear you."

"But the question is, do you believe me?"

There was a long silence. It spoke volumes. Spoke things unsaid. Darius broke the utter silence.

"You're something else, you know that?"

"I've been told."

"Mercedes, what's really up? You can talk to me."

"You ask too many questions. You know that?"

"Do I?"

"Yes."

"Okay, you lead, baby. I'll take it slow and follow your lead."

"I don't know what to talk about now."

"Talk about whatever comes to mind. Just free your mind."

I thought for a moment and listened to his soothing voice. "Darius, you've never told me anything about your family and childhood."

"I haven't, have I?"

He hesitated for only a moment. I could hear him in the background as he adjusted himself in bed. I could picture him fluffing up his pillows and gathering his covers closer, over his near nakedness. He didn't question my sanity. He didn't question my waking him up. He didn't question me. He just talked. And calmed my aching spirit.

Nineteen

When I unlocked the front door and walked into the living room a little after ten o'clock, Miss Betty was already up and about in her wheelchair. She always was an early riser, as long as I could remember. I always joked that Miss Betty was so nosy that she was afraid she'd miss something if she slept late.

Miss Betty had become a pro at easing herself in and out of her wheelchair and navigating around the house. It didn't take much for me to wheelchair proof the house. I just pushed some furniture out of her direct path. It's amazing how one can adjust to a situation.

All I had on my mind was sleep—a comfortable, fluffy pillow and a cozy bed. I was hoping that a few hours of deep, uninterrupted sleep would snap me out of the black funk I was in. I didn't get in these moods often, but when I did, *bam,* I was in serious depression mode. Lately, however, it seemed like those mood swings were occurring closer and closer together.

Miss Betty said the strangest thing when I walked into the kitchen where she was finishing up a bowl of oatmeal with peaches and cream.

"You look like hell. Is that crazy child okay?"

I didn't even have the strength to comment on her name-calling. Not this morning, anyway.

"Yes, ma'am. She'll be okay," I said, taking a bottle of water out the refrigerator.

"From the tidbits I heard from y'alls phone conversation, she has some major man problems."

"Yeah, something like that. But it's resolved now."

"I hope she realizes what a friend she has in you, Mer. I hope she appreciates you."

I didn't speak. It took me a second or two to realize Miss Betty was actually giving me a compliment in her indirect manner.

"Yeah, Mer, you're right. She'll be all right. No matter what she's feeling now, time heals all pain."

"Well, I kept warning her about Jamal's no-good ass. She'll be better off without him anyway. Good for nothing—"

"Mer, that still doesn't diminish what that child is feeling now. Her heart is hurting," Miss Betty said in a whisper, getting a distant gaze in her eyes.

"Mer, I wish you could feel that passionate about someone. Whether you want to admit it or not, passion is what makes us feel alive. Everybody needs to connect with someone on some level. You used to. We used to connect. Somewhere along the way, we lost that connection. I sit and think sometimes about when it happened."

"I think you know the answer to that question already," I barked, whipping my head around to look her square in the eyes.

"Mer, I can't change or turn back the hands of time. I wish I could. I handled that situation the best I knew how."

"Yeah right."

"I did, Mer. I know I haven't always been the best mother to you."

"You got that right," I murmured under my breath. "Whatever, I'm going to bed. I'm tired . . . so very, very tired."

"You do that. Get some rest, Mer. Are you still having those nightmares?"

"Yes, ma'am," I said, walking down the hallway to my bedroom and leaving Miss Betty shaking her head over and over.

After I pulled back the covers and climbed into bed, sleep still evaded me. I tossed and turned for about an hour. I tried counting sheep, I tried going over what I had to do at work on Monday, I tried *not* to think about Shaneeka. I'm not sure when I finally drifted off, but even in sleep, I found no relief. Only pain.

My sleep was dream filled. I dreamed of myself as a child, in the very room I was asleep in. A silent scream invaded my mind and woke me up. After frantically looking around and determining where I was, I realized I was drenched in sweat; the gown I'd managed to put on was soaked and stuck like glue to my back and chest. I silently and thankfully erased any remaining memories of my nightmare. As I trembled uncontrollably and pulled at my sheets, my breathing finally returned to normal.

Since I couldn't sleep anyway, I eased my body out of bed and took a long, hot shower, as hot as I could take it. And then it happened . . . I started crying and couldn't stop the tears that freely ran down my face in long, warm streams. My chest heaved in and out as hard tears escaped. My heart was racing a mile a minute. I imagined this was what a heart attack felt like.

At times like this, I felt like I was losing it completely. I prided myself on being a strong black woman, but at that moment, I felt all alone in the world. No matter how much I tried to deny it, I knew I had felt alone for most of my life. I never felt like I fit in or belonged anywhere. Not as a child, not as a teenager, and not even now, as an adult.

Finally, after huddling in the corner of the shower stall until the water spewed forth freezing cold water, shivering, I found the strength to stand up. I was weak in the knees, so I reached out to hold on to the wall with my right hand. I carefully stepped from the shower, located my red towel, slowly dried myself off, then just stood there looking at the face in the mirror. I remained that way for a while. Just looking at the face in the mirror. Why didn't I feel as wonderful as Darius said I was? Why couldn't I feel? Why couldn't I love myself?

When I finally managed to dress and pull myself together, I ate some toast and drank some hot tea. As a child, when I wasn't feeling well, Miss Betty used to give me that. I still clung to that childhood memory, which brought me comfort.

The remainder of the day was uneventful. The temperature was record high outside. I just tried to stay cool. I called to check on Shaneeka and she sounded awful, but that came as no great surprise. It sounded like she had been crying again.

"Hey, girl."

"Hey."

"How you holding up? Have you had anything to eat?"

"I'm okay and I'm not hungry."

"You sure you all right? You don't sound like it."

"Girl, my home phone started ringing nonstop around seven o'clock this morning."

"What? Well, I guess he made it home," I said, between giggles. "I wish I could have seen his face. And your pissing in the foyer. That was priceless."

"It's not funny, Mer. Jamal was threatening to come over and beat my ass. Girl, he was mad."

"For real?"

"Yeah, girl. What you think? Did you see his place? He cussed me out and said he knew I trashed his place with my partner in crime. He said he knew you had something to do with it too."

"So what? He got what he deserved."

"I had to eventually unplug my home phone and turn off my cell. I just recently turned them back on."

"Jamal hasn't tried to come by or do nothing stupid, has he?"

"No, Melvin is here. And he knows he's here."

"Good. Okay. Just lay low and keep me posted."

"I will. Bye."

Just in case Jamal tried to jump bad, her brother was hanging around her place. Shaneeka's brother, Melvin, was about six-three and 240 pounds of solid muscle. The man had been shot two different times and survived. Shaneeka and I joked that he had nine lives, like a cat. Melvin had been recently released from prison after serving a sentence on robbery charges. Jamal was a dog, but he was no fool.

Twenty

As the evening grew nearer and the sun dropped below the horizon, I picked up the phone several times to cancel my date with Darius, but something stopped me. I figured if I went out and partied, I'd feel better. So eventually I called Darius and asked him to meet me at the jazz club. I gave him directions and hung up. Like before, I insisted on driving separately and meeting him there. He objected, but I didn't give in.

I had to admit that once I started to get ready for my date, my mood took a sharp upward swing. After showering again, I applied my favorite lipstick and a little mascara on my already long eyelashes. My braids were hanging loose, framing my face. When I wore braids, everyone said I looked like a darker version of Vivica Fox, the actress. I thought that was a compliment because Vivica was fierce. The lady was bad. Of all the movies she had appeared in, my favorites were still *Set It Off* and *Soul Food*. No matter what she starred in, Vivica always came across real. I couldn't even hate that the rumor mill proclaimed she'd had a taste of my man 50 Cent. Hey, we could share.

I chose a comfortable pair of pastel pants and a sexy blouse that accented my feminine side. After putting on my favorite pair of fuck me shoes, I was ready to party. A rum and coke was calling my name, and I intended to answer.

I found the Hole, as it was appropriately called, with little to no problems even though I hadn't been there in a while. I immediately spotted Darius's black truck parked in the gravel parking lot as people walked up the narrow entrance. Darius waved and smiled as he saw me pull up and park directly in front of him. As Darius made his way over to my car, I sat and watched him approach. He walked with the stride of a confident black man. I liked that. Liked that a lot. I couldn't hang with a punk-ass, weak-ass piece of a man. Give me a real man any day. Those pretty-boy types, hands as soft as mine, ass-kissing, give-me-a-blonde-with-no-butt, so-called brothers that worked at the bank back at home pissed me off to no limit.

Once Darius got near, I rolled down my window. I even honored him with a smile.

"Hey, beautiful."

"Hey there, yourself."

"Are you ready to go in?" he asked, flashing that sexy smile.

I nodded my head.

"You know, you never told me why you went up to Atlanta," he said, leaning against my car door.

"Nothing to tell. I had to handle some business."

"Did you handle it?"

"You better believe it."

"Good."

I had to secretly laugh because I knew Jamal didn't think it was good right about now. He would see red for a while. Literally. I would have paid to see his face when he walked through that door.

"I enjoyed our conversation this morning; you were different somehow."

"How?"

"I don't know. I guess you let your guard down. You were vulnerable, and I've never seen or heard that side of you before."

"Really?"

"Yes, really, and I liked it. Liked knowing that you could open up and just feel."

"So what are you saying? That I'm cold?"

"No, Mercedes. You always twist my words. I'm just saying that you're usually not emotional. It's like you have a wall up that no one can penetrate. Last night, for just a moment, you let down that brick wall. I'm just glad you chose me to witness it and to confide in."

I didn't know whether to take that as a compliment or not. So, I chose to say nothing and leave it alone.

"You know, it's all right to confide in someone."

"I know."

"Do you? If you allow me, I'm here for you."

I nodded.

As Darius opened my car door for me to step out, I said, "Let's go party, get ripped and then go home and tear off each other's clothes."

Darius laughed because he thought I was kidding. Before the night was over, he'd realize I wasn't.

Twenty-one

From the outside, the Hole was deceiving. It looked like a run-down juke joint in the middle of the Georgia woods. Darius and I actually had to travel down a one-lane dirt road with trees on each side, to reach the Hole. It was definitely one of the best-kept secrets in town. Once inside, it became clear why the place was so popular. The Hole was quaint in a rustic sort of way. The various rooms were so eclectic that they were cool in an offbeat groove. Various styles, themes and colors were all thrown together.

There were three bars in various sections of the club. The large dance floor was in the middle of the spit-polished wood floor and there was an elevated, center stage that was used for Karaoke Tuesdays, Spoken Word Wednesdays and Comic View Thursdays. Tonight there was a local live jazz band that was performing until midnight. After the witching hour, it was hip-hop time. The Hole had the most mouthwatering barbeque riblets that just fell off the bone and rum and cokes that had me not feeling anything. Woo woo, party!

Darius and I had a great time. Hell, it was better than a great time. When we weren't listening to the smooth jazz tunes and whispering into each other's ears, we were dancing our asses off to my man 50 Cent, Sean Paul, Chingy, TI, Usher, Ying Yang Twins

and Beyonce. Darius had some moves on the dance floor that had
me wondering about his moves in bed. Had me checking out his
feet again. They were at least a size eleven or eleven and a half. Woo
woo, party!

I also learned more about the mysterious Darius. I came to the
conclusion that he had his head on straight, which was refreshing.
However, according to him, his wisdom and knowledge didn't
come overnight. There was a time when he ran with the wrong
crowd and did some things he later regretted. According to him,
that stage didn't last long. Maybe my luck was changing after all.
I'd met so many men in the past who weren't about shit. However,
it really didn't matter at the time because I wasn't in it for the long
run myself.

My motto is: Do it to them before they do it to you. I was about
having a good time, still am, but I must admit it was refreshing to
meet someone who could carry on an intelligent conversation and
think past next week. Darius had long-term goals. I was truly feeling him. He had one more test to pass.

Around one a.m., the alcohol I'd consumed had me in another
zone. Sometimes I did that. I'd drink and drink and drink. I knew
that wasn't cool, but drinking made me forget, and sometimes, that
was just what the doctor ordered. Darius was all touchy, feely, super
attentive and he smelled too good. Good enough to eat.

"What cologne are you wearing?"

He smiled at me, setting his beer down on the wooden table
and leaning in closer. "You like?"

I was flirting now, big-time, as I stared into his sexy brown eyes
with those long eyelashes that curled up at the tip. "Yeah, I like, and
I like the man who's wearing it even more."

"Come here."

"Why?"

"Because I said so."

"Ooh, I like a forceful man."

I leaned in even closer, and he whispered, "I like you too. You look very sexy tonight." For some reason, that made me feel good and warm inside. Or maybe it was the liquor. Ha-ha.

This time we kissed. The kiss started out close mouthed and soon accelerated into our tongues playing tug of war with each other.

"It's getting pretty late. Is your mom going to be okay at home by herself?"

"Yeah, she's probably sleeping by now," I said, looking at my watch. "Besides, she has friends who check up on her when I'm not there."

"Cool. Are you having a good time?"

"Yes, I am. I really am. This place is wild."

"Good. You look like it. You're glowing."

I glanced down at my watch again so he wouldn't see me blush. "Where has the time gone?"

"What do you want to do? Dance some more, or grab a bite to eat somewhere?" Darius asked, lifting my hand and placing a light kiss on top of it.

A mischievous look crossed my face. "Come here."

Darius leaned in again, and I turned my body so that I could whisper in his ear and be up close and personal.

"I want you to take me home and make love to me. Can you do that?"

"I think I can handle that request," he said, gingerly taking my hand and leading me to the exit and into the early-morning coolness. A new day was upon us.

Once at my car, we were soon engaged in another round of kissing and caressing. When Darius squeezed my left breast, I felt dancing butterflies in my stomach. I lowered his hand down so that he'd know what was in store for him. I saw his eyes cast over in desire when his fingers touched my spot.

Twenty-two

It took me over ten minutes to convince Darius I was capable of driving. After trailing Darius back to town, very slowly and on the lookout for the police the entire time, I soon learned that his home was the basement of his mother's house. When we pulled up, I saw a blue four-door sedan parked out front. The house itself was modest: brick with green trim and a small front yard with freshly mowed grass. There was a bed of roses on the far side of the front steps.

"Whose car is that? Whose house is this?" I asked, looking around to take in my surroundings with unfocused, squinted eyes.

"That's my mother's car, and this is her house. I guess I didn't tell you that I lived with her, did I?" Darius asked, looking away.

"No, I guess you left out that part," I said in a smartass, sassy tone. All sorts of thoughts were going through my mind, like, *Why did this grown-ass man live with his mama?*

"Well, this is only temporary. After my divorce, my financial situation was pretty jacked up. I had creditors calling me left and right, night and day, at home and at work. So until I could get back on my feet, I moved in with my mother, at her request. I live in the basement and pay her rent each month and help out around the place. You know, fixing up things here and there."

"Okay."

"I guess you could say I'm learning to crawl before I can walk again."

I could tell this was making Darius a bit uncomfortable. For the first time, I saw a glimpse of that macho image he portrayed slipping.

"Is this setup okay with you? If not, we can leave. Go to a hotel or something."

"No, I'm cool. I just wish you had told me earlier. I don't like surprises. I like to know what I'm walking into."

"If you're worried about privacy, I have my own entrance and exit. My mother respects my privacy and vice versa. She wouldn't think of coming downstairs."

I placed my finger over his lips. "Stop all the talking and let's go in so you can show me what you got, big boy," I playfully said, grabbing his crotch and feeling more than a handful.

Darius smiled and the tension between us instantly vanished. We'd leaped that hurdle successfully. Once Darius unlocked the door to the basement and ushered me in, I found myself timid for a moment. I looked around and my eyes adjusted to the dim lighting, and I had to admit, Darius had good taste. His place looked like a bachelor pad, but everything was in bold, vivid colors. His space was inviting, pulled you in. Just like him.

Across one wall were just bookcases and bookcases of books. Hardcover. Paperback. Self-help. Nonfiction. Religious. Autobiographies of our great black leaders. I was impressed. Most of the men I had been with in the past, about the only thing you'd catch them reading was *Playboy* or the sports section of the newspaper.

Darius saw me checking out his books. "Knowledge is power, baby."

Darius took a couple of steps and turned on a small lamp over by the end table and asked me if I wanted anything to drink.

"No, I just want you. Let me slurp you up."

Darius didn't say another word. He simply walked over to me, reached for my left hand and led me down the narrow hallway to his bedroom. Once he placed me on his queen-size bed, Darius walked to the foot of his bed and I watched him undress, inch by inch. Ever so slowly. He was putting on a strip show just for me, and I was front row and center. Just as I thought, he had a beautiful, sculptured body. He said he didn't work out, but I guess his job kept him in great shape. His manhood was impressive as well. By now it was at full attention. The entire time Darius was undressing, he never took his eyes off me. As I reclined on his pillow, I was hypnotized. Hell, I was mesmerized.

When Darius finished disrobing and was standing like a bronze God in front of me, he reached for me. I instantly gasped as shivers ran up and down my body. Darius proceeded to undress me piece by piece. Like he was undressing a baby. There was so much tenderness, care and love in each touch. As each item of my clothing landed on the floor and left behind another piece of my nakedness, his eyes revealed that he liked what he saw. The only sounds were our labored breathing and the stillness of the night. Crickets were our symphony.

I was suddenly unsure of myself. I didn't know if it was the alcohol or what, but I felt strange. Emotions were stirring inside me that I had never experienced before. I felt light-headed. For once, I didn't feel in control.

I spoiled the moment by jumping his bones. At first Darius was shocked, taken off guard. Then he kinda laid back and went with the flow as I climbed on top of him and rode that wild stallion like there was no tomorrow. I started out slow, and then I picked up the pace as he started to feel better than good. My braids were wild and flying all over the place, my eyes gazed over, and I was working that thang. Worked it well.

I was the captain of that ship and all I could think of was completing my fantastic voyage. Darius tried to touch me a few times, but I placed his arms up near his head, and he got the message. Finally, I came. I came hard. It took moments for me to calm back down. After I pleased myself, Darius pushed me off of him right away. I didn't care. I had gotten mine.

"Now, let's start again, Mer."

"What do . . . ?"

"Sshh, don't say anything," he said, placing his finger over my lips.

"Just lay back and let me show you how much I like you. Let me please you. I'm the man, and I want to make love to you, not have hurried sex. Let's do this slow and easy."

I guess he saw a hint of fear in my eyes. And I did notice that he'd called me by my nickname. As he touched the heat between my legs, I trembled.

"Mer, I'm not going to hurt you. Trust me. Let go and trust me. Let go. Free your mind."

As he slowly pushed two fingers inside me and massaged my clit with his thumb, I strained to hold in a moan.

Darius looked down at me with such love and tenderness. "Let it go."

Darius touched me again. I moaned out in raw, uncontrollable ecstasy.

"Lay all the way back, close your eyes and enjoy, baby."

I laid there in anticipation as Darius started from the top of my head and slowly inched his way downward. Every spot received love and attention. My eyelids were kissed with reckless abandon until I honored his request to close them. When he reached my mouth, I turned away. I still didn't enjoy kissing. Taking someone's tongue and saliva into your mouth. Yuck. Earlier, the drinks had caused me to indulge in kissing.

Darius slowly pulled me back to him and kissed me gently and then with greater passion and urgency. His tongue was introducing itself to my mouth. Once I surrendered and gave in to the sensations, I started to enjoy myself. Darius was still inching his way downward. My twin mounds were experiencing the joy now.

All kinds of thoughts were running through my head and breaking through my alcohol-induced haze. Darius was softly whispering all sorts of sweet nothings to me. Telling me how sexy I was, how beautiful I looked, how good I felt. When he kissed my stomach and stuck his warm tongue into my belly button, chills went up and down my arms. When I tried to touch him, he gently, but firmly, pushed my hands away, placed them above my head.

He traveled farther down to my inner thighs. I was visibly shaking and moaning. He looked up once and said he wanted to taste me, right before he bent my legs and spread them as wide as they would go. When his lips and tongue made contact with my womanhood, I tried to pull away. It was feeling too good. I didn't deserve this love, this caring.

Darius didn't release his grip, and in no time at all I was seeing the heaven and stars, the universe. When the spastic motions finally ceased and my breathing was almost back to normal, Darius slowly and teasingly entered me.

"Open your eyes and look at me, Mer."

As his thrusts increased in intensity and deepness, I couldn't take it anymore. Fireworks went off throughout my being. And afterwards, as Darius held me and stroked my hair, I did the craziest thing: I cried. I cried softly into his shoulder as he held me and comforted me with warm touches and caresses. Words weren't necessary. Our lovemaking had spoken volumes.

Twenty minutes later, I was ready to book; I was so embarrassed. I had to get a grip. What was this man doing to me?

"Darius, the crying . . . I'm sorry. I'm just tired and I have a lot going on in my life right now."

"Listen, it's okay. You don't have to explain. Did it feel good?"

"Yes, it did. Unbelievable."

"Good. I wanted to show you what I feel for you."

As I stared at the rust-colored bedspread, I said, "I have to go." I couldn't even look at Darius. I sensed him staring at me as he smoothed down my braids.

"Now?"

"Yeah, Miss Betty might need me."

"I thought you said she was okay for the night. I assumed you could spend the night with me. I'd love to wake up with you next to me. See your sweet face first thing in the morning."

"No, I have to go," I repeated, stumbling around blindly in the dark, looking for my clothes. Anxious to cover my nakedness, I dressed hurriedly.

"Well, let me walk you to your car," Darius said with a confused expression on his face.

"No, you don't have to."

"Mer, I know, but I want to," he said, pulling his pants back on. I looked away.

It seemed like it took forever to make it to my car. My mind was spinning in a million different directions. I was hoping and praying that I didn't start crying again like a fool.

Darius opened my car door for me to get in and leaned inside my open window. Our scents still clung to each other.

"When can I see you again?"

"I don't know. You really want to see me after tonight? I know you think I'm crazy or something. Crying and shit."

"No, I don't think you're crazy. You have a lot going on in your life: sick mother, job woes. I'll call you, okay?"

"Cool," I said, turning the key in my ignition.

"Mer, remember what I told you. I'm not going to beg you. You have to want me the way I need you. Tonight meant something to me."

When he leaned in to kiss me, I didn't turn my head away. As our saliva mixed and his tongue claimed a small spot in my heart, I quickly said good night again as my eyes began to water up. What was going on with me? What was this man doing to me? Maybe I was finally losing my mind. Darius told me to drive safely. As I drove off like a bat out of hell, I glanced back in the rearview mirror. He was standing in the middle of the street, no shirt on and a pair of black pants, watching me drive off. For some reason that I can't quite put my finger on, that bothered me. Bothered me a lot.

Twenty-three

After my strange behavior, Darius and I did hook up again. Much to my surprise, I found myself picking up the phone to speak with him a week later. I made a point of not going to church that Sunday after our second date because I didn't want to see him. I knew Darius would take one look in my face and see how much he had affected me. He had me crying and shit.

Hell, I was still getting used to these new feelings and accepting them myself. Once I made the decision that I was willing to take our relationship to another level, one day at a time, to see where it went, Darius and I became inseparable.

Amazingly, the scorching summer was flying by. Already, I was into the sixth week since I'd been back home. Miss Betty was out of her wheelchair and walking around a few minutes each day and did her exercises with a curse word or complaint after each stretch. She passed her checkups with flying colors. Our love-hate relationship continued, and sometimes I'd catch her staring at me when she thought I wasn't looking. I have no idea what she was searching for when she studied me so intensely.

Believe it or not, sometimes we talked and laughed—yes, actually laughed—about my childhood antics. I was a pure tomboy. I could play basketball, softball and football with the best of the neighborhood boys. One evening Miss Betty and I pulled out this old battered and worn photo album and checked out pictures that seemed ancient. Those were a trip. We laughed and laughed and laughed as we ate buttery microwave popcorn.

I came across a very old photo of the daddy I never knew. He died from a drug overdose when I was three months old. At times like that, I could feel fleeting waves of love that I wanted to hang on to no matter how short-lived. I used to wonder and dream about what it would have been like to grow up with a daddy in the house. Miss Betty didn't talk about him a lot, so finally I forgot I ever had one.

Miss Betty was the only father and mother that I ever knew. According to her, the only one I ever needed. As a child, sometimes, I'd get jealous when a neighborhood child talked about something that she and her dad did over the weekend. But growing up, the majority of the children I knew didn't have fathers in their homes either.

Shaneeka did it, she actually threw Jamal to the curb. I just knew she was going to take his ass back. Would have bet money on it. Yet she proved me wrong. She met a nice young man, and they are happily dating. According to Shaneeka, he's not as good as Jamal in bed and doesn't have a lot of money, but he treats her like a lady, opens doors for her and everything. I'll see what happens. I hope this nice young man isn't just a distraction for her.

Guess who called me the other night? Redman. It was basically a two a.m. booty call, but I surprised myself by declining his offer. I hung up, turned over and went back to sleep. There was a time when I would have been over there in a hot minute with my bag of tricks in tow.

Work was still work. What could I say though? It paid the bills.

My coworkers had gotten used to me by now. So they knew the deal. I was professional most of the time, yet cross me and I'd go off on their asses, and they'd see my true ghetto side. Believe it or not, I'd even gone out to lunch with a few of the women. Jennifer and Ashley were not so bad if you took them in small doses. I'd even acquired some favorite customers of my own. They preferred me to answer their questions and research their concerns. They'd even wait a few extra minutes just to speak with me. That small gesture made me feel like my job was worthwhile. So, all in all, the summer was turning out better than I expected. Of course, Darius had a lot to do with it.

For this entire week, I had been an emotional wreck. Darius wanted me to meet his mom, Ruth, on Sunday. I was literally terrified. In all my thirty years, I had never met a man's mom. For what? I wasn't going to be around four to five months down the line. For the first time, I wondered what it'd feel like to be in a long-term relationship.

As more and more time went by, I realized Darius was different. Different in a good way. Different in a way I had never seen or experienced before. Darius had made my summer as well as made me question, for the first time, some of my theories on love and relationships. Could I have been wrong? Were marriage and children in my future?

With Darius, I discovered I could let my guard down and he'd have my back. He didn't judge me. In fact, he gave me a lot of sound, solid advice about dealing with Miss Betty. Redman did all that as well. However, there was one big difference: I wasn't falling in love with Redman.

Darius now knew that Miss Betty and I had a love-hate rela-

tionship going on. He had even met her when he came by one
evening to pick me up. Yeah, he was even doing that. We were no
longer driving separate cars on dates. My baby picked me up and
even opened the car door for me.

Of course, Miss Betty asked a million questions and charmed
him with her wit. She could be charming when she wanted to be.
However, it made it seem like I was exaggerating or lying about
her because I never saw that charm or wit when we were alone.

And vice versa. Darius was a true gentleman to Miss Betty. He
even brought her flowers. When I first opened the front door to
his smiling face, I thought they were for me, and he turned around
and handed the bouquet of flowers over to Miss Betty and listened
to her crazy stories and gossip like they were interesting. Miss Betty
broke it down to him on everybody at church and had him laughing his ass off. Darius was an instant hit, and I was secretly pleased
that they hit it off so well. Miss Betty also especially liked the fact
that Darius had never been to jail, didn't do drugs, had a job and
was a decent man.

Darius and I had had many late-night phone conversations even
though both of us knew we needed to get up early the next morning for work. I loved it when I'd be thinking about him, the phone
would ring, and he'd be on the line. Made me feel like we were
connected. I was still amazed at how I opened up to him. Once I
started, it was like a floodgate had opened and my truths rushed
forward into the murky waters. Some of my truths made me pon-
der decisions I had made earlier on. Yet Darius didn't judge. He just
loved me as I was, flaws and all.

I had never been one to verbally express my true feelings to
anyone, even Shaneeka, and we told each other everything. I told
Darius how different I felt growing up with a mama who was bi-

sexual. For most of my life, I'd always felt different. As a child, I was always trying to fit in, but I never found that perfect fit. After a while, I stopped trying and realized I was who I was. Accept me or don't. Still, I wondered if I had accepted myself. I knew for sure, though, that sometimes I didn't like myself.

Twenty-four

Getting back to Miss Betty, growing up, I never knew who she'd bring home. I was always holding my breath, walking around on eggshells and waiting for the next surprise. For a brief time during my college years, I questioned by own sexuality. Yeah, I had a hot and steamy relationship with a woman for four months before I realized that wasn't what I was about. Devon—that was her name—was not on the bisexual curve. She knew she craved women and only women. Devon saw something in me during my junior year, and she set out to seduce me. And guess what? She succeeded. Once we were thrown together as study partners for a marketing class project, it was easy.

Devon was intelligent, gorgeous, with curly auburn hair, wore the latest fashions and had an upper-class upbringing. Yeah, totally different from me with my meager food allowance and second-hand clothing. I was at Albany State on scholarship, and just like at home, I was poor. I couldn't indulge in any luxuries. Hell, I still couldn't. I didn't live the American dream. Only a paycheck separated me from those living on the streets.

On the other hand, Devon's family actually owned a summer home off the coast of North Carolina. She lived off campus in her own fully furnished apartment. I lived on campus because it was part of my scholarship. Many evenings, after dinner, we'd meet at her apartment instead of the library and study into the late night or the early morning. I soon got into the habit of bringing an overnight bag and spending the night. Sure, I knew of her sexual preference, but I also knew that we were only study partners. Besides, living with Miss Betty, I was used to not discriminating against others society deemed different. Hell, I was different.

One Friday night after drinking too much wine and smoking too much weed, it happened. We were sitting around in our underwear and long T-shirts and giggling like two high-school girls. Devon said in that sweet, sexy voice of hers, "You have a great body, Mercedes. You know that?"

I giggled, and I never giggled. "You have it going on yourself, and you don't even work at it. All that junk food you consume every day doesn't put a pound on you."

Devon leaned over to grab the almost-empty bottle of wine off the mahogany coffee table. She stumbled a little and fell back against the soft leather sofa cushion.

"Want some more?" she asked, shaking the bottle and looking inside.

I shook my head and Devon placed the bottle back on the table. For the first time, I took an inventory of Devon and noticed how sexy she actually was. She was a natural beauty and exuded just the right amount of sexuality. She didn't have that so-called butch look that a lot of lesbians possessed. If I were a man, I'd want some of that.

Devon came out of the blue with her next question. "Have you ever kissed a woman?" she asked, staring straight at me for my reaction.

As I noticed her dark nipples straining against her T-shirt, I swallowed, looked up and shook my head again. No expression crossed my face. By now I was used to masking my true feelings. I knew where this was leading.

"Have you ever thought about it?" Devon asked, leaning back with her legs slightly open. I could see the dark, curly outline of her patch through her black silk panties.

"Have you ever thought about it? About how it would feel?"

"No. I don't know. I guess every woman has wondered about it at some point. Wonders what it's like to love herself."

"Don't you want to satisfy your curiosity?"

I hesitated, uncertain. Yet the wine was giving me courage and making me bold. Very bold.

"Sure. Why not? I'll try anything once."

Devon searched my face for a quick second, reached for me with her long, delicate, slender fingers, and as her softness meshed into mine, our lips, then our urgent tongues, performed their own dance ritual. Devon was very feminine. However, she was definitely a coochie eater. When Devon touched my breasts, my entire body responded. This surprised me. I thought I wouldn't be able to get into it with a woman. Wrong.

She knew instinctively where my hot spots were. And I also noticed how gentle and loving she was. Foreplay lasted longer with Devon than with any man I had been with. Before the night was over, the simple kiss had gone from passionate to my legs bent back to my head while her tongue had me speaking in foreign languages and dialogues.

From that point on, it was on. Devon would be eating from the plate whenever we had time together, which was often. We'd barely make it into her apartment before our clothes would be strewn from the living room to the bedroom. My legs would spread the minute they touched the bed and Devon would go to work.

Devon used to say that she loved seeing my eyes glaze over right before I was came. It made her work harder.

Our relationship lasted roughly four months before the novelty wore off and I realized I needed a hard dick on my plate. We went our separate ways. Devon taught me a valuable lesson; I wasn't my mama. Again, after hearing this confession, Darius didn't judge me.

Twenty-five

Talking late into the night became our ritual. He acted as my personal therapist as I beared my soul and aired my dirty laundry. To my amazement, my revelations didn't make me weak; they did the opposite: made me stronger. We got into the habit of having quick lunches at least once or twice each week. Sometimes we grabbed a quick burger and rode out to a nearby park with a lake view to eat and enjoy each other's company.

A couple of times, we drove up to Atlanta for long weekends and to visit Shaneeka. We'd hang out at the mall, attend various music festivals going on that particular weekend or check out the local clubs. We even had a picnic at Stone Mountain Park. Darius enjoyed himself but admitted that he didn't really enjoy the hustle and bustle of city living. I was changing. I could feel myself achieving more inner peace. With each revelation, I was elevated to a higher level of peace. Even my nightmares had started to subside.

For the first time ever, I was considering a future that included a husband and perhaps children. Yes, I now had dreams of settling down. Love was no longer some unattainable myth. It was real. It was real because I was feeling it in my heart each and every day for Darius.

I knew so much about Darius and his earlier years that I felt like I had grown up with him. He was a great storyteller and he kept me in stitches most of the time. I had never laughed so much in my life as I did when I finally chose to open up my heart. Like me, Darius was raised by a single mom, but unlike me, he had a happy, uneventful childhood. His childhood was normal. A few cuts and bruises, but nothing tragic.

His mom had three older brothers, and they kept Darius in line with love and switches. According to Darius, they basically made him the man he was today: not afraid of hard work, providing for his family, giving back to the community and trying to be the best person he could be. I admired that.

During his childhood, Darius was the all-American boy—sports, girls and partying occupied his young-adult years. As a young man, he served ten years in the army. After his stint in the service, he returned home and married his childhood sweetheart, Latrice, who eventually got strung out on crack cocaine. Before Darius even realized the extent of her drug usage, it was too late. I could sense the pain still fresh in his voice when he spoke of Latrice. I think he felt that he failed her in some way.

Darius said that to this day he didn't know how Latrice started using. He thought her cousin may have introduced her to it. The marriage slowly dissolved because Latrice didn't try to help herself, much less let Darius help her. He lost everything: his house and his sanity. Now two years later, he was still trying to piece his life slowly back together. UPS provided a steady paycheck to repair his bad credit. He admitted he enjoyed married life, and his ex hadn't soured him on the institute of matrimony. He wanted home ownership along with a wife and children someday. He wanted the American dream. Darius was a dreamer. I, however, was a realist.

Darius admitted that he still loved Latrice, just wasn't in love with her. He cared about her deeply. After all, she was his first love. Yet he couldn't forgive her for the torment and hell she put him through. However, I felt assured she was his past. Distant past.

Darius and his mom were close. Very close. Yeah, he was a mama's boy and proud of it. Secretly I somewhat envied their close relationship. When he talked of his mom, his voice got softer, dreamier and gentler. His entire demeanor changed. Every Sunday she and Darius sat down to a large dinner that she lovingly prepared. It was usually too much for just the two of them, but that was their ritual.

He loved her with all his heart. I respected that. And on the day before I was to meet her, be a part of this ritual, their relationship scared me. I mean, what if she thought I wasn't good enough for her son? What if she didn't like me? What if she sensed I wasn't good at loving someone?

Twenty-six

As Darius and I walked up the sidewalk to the dark green front door, my stomach bubbled like it was alive with a thousand butterflies fluttering in every direction in hopes of escaping. As for me, I wanted to disappear like Jeannie on *I Dream of Jeannie*. When I was a child, I wanted that power so bad. To be able to disappear at will.

Today I was dressed casually in a pair of blue slacks, a light blue blouse and sling-back shoes. I figured today was not the day for my hoochie-mama attire.

Darius must have realized my distress because he smiled in my direction and caressed my hair to assure me that everything would be okay. I touched his dimple. I had been to his mama's house many times. However, I always entered through the basement entrance, never through the front door. I had seen photos of her, but in just a few moments I'd be face-to-face with the real thing. Mrs. Ruth Dargon.

Darius opened the front door with his key and called out to his mom. "Mama, we're here."

I quickly and quietly checked out my surroundings and immediately noticed the homely, inviting feel to the house. Everything was nice and neat and felt well lived in. There were many photos of Darius in various stages of his life. All happy, smiling photos of him at different ages. Photos of him in grade school with missing teeth, photos of him older, with a big Afro, photos of him as captain of the football team, photos of him on prom night with his arms wrapped around his petite, pretty date. I checked them all out and realized what a wonderful life he'd had. The pictures told the story. There was no sorrow in this house. No pain here. Only the joy of living and loving.

The living room was decorated in hues of blues and burgundy with a few prints on the walls. A recliner sat in the far corner of the living room, and the fireplace mantel displayed various knickknacks of different animals made out of crystal. A small TV was in front of the navy sofa, but it was turned off.

I heard light footsteps heading our way, so I prepared my expression with an inviting smile.

"Mercedes, so nice to finally meet you. I've heard so much about you," a tall, medium-built lady who was the female spitting image of Darius said, pulling me into a light embrace.

"Mrs. Dargon, it's nice meeting you as well," I said, gently pulling away.

"No, please call me Ruth. Everyone else does," she said, looking me up and down from head to toe with a critical eye.

"Okay . . . Ruth. You have a lovely home. Very cozy."

"Thank you. I'm very happy here. We've been in this house for over thirty years. This house is older than Darius."

She smiled.

I smiled.

"I was just putting the final touches on dinner; Mercedes will you come in the kitchen and help me finish up?"

I looked over at Darius and he was smiling, looking at me and then back to his mom like a little boy. He was thoroughly enjoying this.

"Sure."

"Darius, I know there has to be a game or something on the tube. Sit down. Relax. Mercedes will be okay with me. Don't worry. I don't bite."

We made our way into the sunny kitchen, which faced out into their backyard, and wonderful smells greeted my nostrils. Darius had told me that his mom was an excellent cook, that she considered herself a chef of sorts. If she watched TV, it was usually a cooking show. He said that Ruth was always trying something new and cutting out recipes from food magazines and the newspaper.

"Something smells good in here. I hear you are a wonderful cook."

"Did Darius tell you that?"

"Yes, ma'am."

She smiled like I'd told her she had won the lottery or something. "I hope you're a good cook too because that man in there can eat you out of house and home. Whew. I don't know where he puts it."

"Well, so far, I haven't had the opportunity to cook for him."

"Why not? Hasn't your mama told you that the way to a man's heart is his stomach?" she teased, looking up from what she was doing.

I started to say something really smart at that moment, but I chose to remain silent. "I guess she didn't."

"Well, I guess I'm a little old-fashioned compared to some of today's standards. I'm just a country girl at heart."

I smiled.

"Okay, the food is almost done. I just need to take my corn bread out of the oven in a few minutes. In the meantime, you can help me set the table."

I smiled as she handed me some pink and blue flowered china plates that were trimmed in gold. As I looked around, I noticed

tons of cookbooks on the white baker's rack sitting over in the corner by the large bay window. The window provided a view of the
entire backyard.

"You know, Darius talks about you nonstop."

"I hope it's all good," I teased in a half-joking manner.

"Oh yes, he thinks highly of you, dear."

"That's good to know."

I placed a plate on the place mat, and Ruth followed behind me
and set the gold-plated flatware down.

"You know this is the first time since his divorce . . . You do
know that he's divorced?"

"Yes, he told me all about that unfortunate situation."

"Anyway, as I was saying, this is the first time since his divorce
that my son has brought a woman home for me to meet. He hasn't
really dated much since that tragedy."

She paused for emphasis.

"Darius and Latrice were so happy together, made the perfect
couple and they had their entire futures ahead of them. What a
shame," she said, shaking her head. "So sad."

I simply nodded and smiled. I didn't know what else to do as
she handed me the glassware.

"What do you think of my son?"

That question threw me for a moment. I was already getting
sick of playing fifty questions with mommy dearest. "I think Darius is wonderful. He's a good and decent man."

"Really? Most young women today are not into the good guys.
Seems like all they want is a thug with some money who will slap
'em around and show 'em no respect."

"Well, from what I can see, Darius is definitely one of the good
guys. He's been through a lot, and it hasn't soured him on relationships. He's a good man."

"Yes, he has," Mrs. Dargon said, getting caught up in her own thoughts. "And yes, he's a very good man. I'm very proud of my son. That's why I was so surprised that he brought you home after knowing you for such a brief period of time," Mrs. Dargon said, glancing at me from the corner of her eye.

"Well, I think we hit it off well right away."

"Uh-huh, that's good. I wouldn't want him to be hurt again."

"Well, Mrs. Dargon, I have no plans of hurting him in any way, shape, form or fashion."

"Understand, I'm very protective of Darius, and like you said, he has been through a lot these past few years. He's only recently healed."

"Well, that's understandable, but from what I've seen, he is a grown man and he can take care of himself," I said in my most nonconfrontational tone.

Mrs. Dargon stopped filling the water glasses and looked at me. I guess she didn't know how to take my last comment. "So we have an understanding?"

"Excuse me?" I asked in total confusion.

"I said, do we have an understanding? An understanding that Darius has been through enough drama. I'm sure you wouldn't bring any more drama into his life."

Darius chose that moment to enter the kitchen. There is a God.

"Mama, I had to check on you two. There's no telling what you're saying to Mercedes up in here," he joked, walking over and placing his arms around my waist.

"Baby, we are just getting to know each other better. Aren't we, Mercedes?" she asked, winking in my direction.

"Yes, ma'am," I responded without the wink.

After checking out the table setting, Mrs. Dargon was satisfied because she asked us to wash our hands and have a seat. Dinner was served.

Twenty-seven

Darius was so right. His mom could cook her ass off. However, I couldn't totally enjoy the meal because Mrs. Dargon continued to ask me a million damn questions.

"So, Mercedes, what do you do for a living, dear? Mercedes, what does your mother do for a living? Do you own a house or apartment back in Atlanta? When will you be leaving for Atlanta? What high school and college did you attend?"

"Mama, let her come up for air. This isn't fifty questions."

"Yes, you're right. Seconds, dear?"

I shook my head. I was just ready to leave.

"Is the food not up to your expectations?"

"No, it's great. I'm just not very hungry. I had a large lunch earlier."

"Well, Mercedes, you shouldn't eat a big meal before coming to a dinner. Remember that next time."

I dropped my fork, a little too loudly. I silently counted from ten to one. "You're right."

That was my formal introduction to Mrs. Dargon. Darius and his mom chatted back and forth about what was going on in the neighborhood. They were implementing a neighborhood watch program in which Mrs. Dargon would chair. She told me stories of Darius's adolescent years. I listened and threw in a few fake smiles for good measure. I had never smiled so much before in my life; I wasn't a smiler. However, I was just thankful that she was off my back for a while. My reprieve didn't last long because by dessert, Mrs. Dargon was back on my case.

"Mercedes, how old are you, if I may ask?"

"I'm thirty."

"That's good. Darius is thirty-two." I nodded like this was news to me.

"Have you ever been married?"

"No, I haven't," I said, clearing my throat a little too loudly.

"Why not? A pretty girl like you should have lots of admirers knocking at your door."

I chose to remain silent and pretended to chew the last remnants of my sweet potato pie, which was off the chart. Mrs. Dargon, or Ruth, as she preferred to be called, put her foot in it. "Well?"

"Excuse me?"

"Why haven't you been married before?"

Darius chose that moment to perform a timely intervention. I silently rubbed his foot with my heel from under the table to thank him. Darius had warned me about his mama. As much as he loved her, she was a bit of a meddler. I had determined that a bit of a meddler was an understatement. This lady was all up in my Kool-Aid. I tried to remember that this was her love for her son speaking. However, she was getting on my last good nerve.

By the time we had washed the dishes and made our way into the living room, I was all fake smiled out and ready to end the torture. Going upstairs to use the bathroom and sneaking kisses from Darius before coming back down lifted my spirits some. However, Mrs. Dargon had one final bit of info to spill. Unfortunately, this info didn't bring a smile to my face for the rest of the evening.

"Mrs. Dargon, thanks so much for the wonderful meal. It was

great meeting you today," I said, anxiously standing to my feet and reaching for my purse.

"Are y'all getting ready to rush out already?"

"Yeah, Mom, we are checking out a movie over at the Rialto."

"Well, I know I won't see you until sometime tomorrow. So let me give you this message before I forget again. Latrice called and wants you to call her back about meeting with her about temporary visitation arrangements for Shelby."

As he glanced over at his mom, I saw Darius's face tense up into a scowl. I quickly looked from Darius back to his mom. I was hearing bull, and it smelled like shit.

"Latrice? Isn't that your ex-wife, Darius? And who is Shelby?" I asked, trying to control the tone of my voice.

"Yeah, baby that's my ex. Latrice is back in town."

"Back in town?" I shouted a little too loudly. "Since when?"

"Yeah, rumor has it she's cleaned up her act."

"How—when—were you planning to tell me this?"

"Baby, let's talk about this later. Okay?"

"No, Darius, it's not okay!" I screamed back.

"Mer, she's been back for only a few days. I'm still adjusting to the news myself."

In my wave of questions, I had totally forgotten about Mrs. Dargon. She may as well have been invisible. I looked over at Mrs. Dargon who was sitting in her high-back chair with what looked like a slight smirk on her face. She was taking this all in.

"Well, you should have told me a few days ago. And who is Shelby?"

Darius lowered his head as if he wanted to shrink through the living room floor. I could tell he wanted to be anywhere but in the same room with me and his mom. After she answered my question, I shared his pain.

"Mer, hasn't Darius told you? I thought you said he told you everything, dear. Shelby is my granddaughter; Darius's four-year-old daughter."

"Excuse me. His what?" I asked, taking a seat on the sofa so I wouldn't pass out.

I know my mouth hit the floor because I vaguely remember picking it up. I was beside pissed off; I was ballistic. I wanted to slap the black off Darius and slap that stupid smirk his mom wore so elegantly through the wooden floor. How dare he make a complete fool of me . . . and in front of his mom? Lying, no-good, making-me-believe in love, motherfucka.

I needed air. I was suffocating. I had to get out of there before I slapped the shit out of both of them. I admit Darius looked devastated, but his mom looked like she was pleased with the results of this piece of info that had been divulged.

"I have to go. Now!" I said, standing up too quickly. How could I be so stupid and think he was different? Stupid me.

"So soon?"

"Yes, I have the beginnings of a migraine."

"Okay, dear, go home, take some aspirin, and get some rest."

"Okay, baby, I'll take you home and explain all this. I promise."

I somehow made it to his truck, got in and maintained a stupid, goofy smile on my face until we were out of view of his mom who stood in the doorway waving like June Cleaver on *Leave It to Beaver*. Darius broke the painful silence.

"Mer, I'm sorry you had to find out this way."

"You have a daughter, and your ex is back in town? I can't fucking believe this shit. You've never mentioned a daughter before. Why?" I asked, feeling tears flood my eyes. I quickly wiped them away. Darius didn't deserve my tears.

Darius leaned over to touch my knee.

"Don't you *dare* touch me!" I screamed between gritted teeth. "Don't you *dare*!"

"Mer, you're overreacting. Let me explain." Pain was etched all over his handsome face.

"You couldn't tell me before, I don't want to know now. I'm not interested in your baby mama drama. Just take my black ass home and go find your wife and child."

"Mer?"

"What part of don't talk to me do you not understand?" I said, looking him up and down with hateful, spiteful eyes.

Darius just rubbed his head and shut up.

The rest of the drive was made in complete, utter silence as I looked out the window and saw absolutely nothing. I couldn't stand to see his face or breathe the same air as him. When we arrived at my house, I jumped out the truck and slammed the door as hard as I could. I wanted to knock it off its hinges. I leaned into the passenger window with hell's fury outlined in every pore of my face.

"FORGET MY NUMBER! FORGET YOU EVER KNEW ME! UNDERSTAND THAT, MR. DARGON?"

Darius didn't say anything; he knew at that point I was beyond an explanation, and anything rational was beyond my reach.

"Oh, and one more thing. Thanks for proving, once again, that you men are all the damn same. Sorry as hell."

Twenty-eight

I had never felt pain like that before in my entire life. Pain that felt like it had a grip on my heart and was ripping my insides out after being stomped on with steel shoes. I had never shed so many tears. Rivers and rivers of tears behind closed doors. This pain, which was new to me, was gut-wrenching, made me want to get down on bended knees, throw my hands towards the heavens and howl like a baby who had a bad case of colic.

I'd never felt so vulnerable and betrayed before in my life. But you know what? That's what I get. That's what I get for letting my guard down. I knew my rules; I could play the game. I should have followed them. Hell, I had to catch feelings for the man. But never again! I mean, his mom, of all people, had to tell me about his ex and daughter. A daughter?

Every time I closed my eyes I pictured the smug look I had on my face when I explained to Mrs. Dargon how her son told me everything; we had no secrets. We were open and honest with each other. Why didn't he tell me this shit? I could even deal with his wife—excuse me, ex-wife—being back in town because I didn't feel threatened in the least little bit. The hell she put him through with her crack-addicted self, stealing anything for her next fix, I'll suck your dick for a hit, he'd be crazy to want to reconnect, recommit and give it one more try with her. But not telling me about his daughter now, that was another story. Ex-wives can come and go, but your son or daughter is forever; that's blood. And forever is a long time when the ex is in the picture as well.

I had thought of every possible scenario as to why Darius didn't or couldn't tell me about his daughter. In the end, it didn't matter. Bottom line, it came as a complete and utter surprise to me. Darius talked about wanting a serious relationship with me, mentioned marriage, us having a future together, but he couldn't tell me this. It didn't make sense. No matter what angle you viewed it, the shit didn't make sense.

All I know is that the nigga betrayed my trust, which you don't gain easily, and quickly verified my initial theory on men. No good, low-down, motherfuckers. I knew I should have just fucked him and called it a day. Now I was walking around like I had lost my best friend on earth, in the universe. And I disgusted myself with the way I carried on. Absolutely pathetic.

Last week, I couldn't believe I sat there and cried on the phone to Shaneeka for hours. Hours, you hear me. My long-distance bill was going to be ridiculous. And you know what? She never said he played me or rubbed it in my face. Shaneeka is my girl. Yet I knew that anyway. She was even going to take some vacation days, come and visit to cheer me up. I told her not to because secretly I couldn't bear her seeing me at my lowest.

Shaneeka thought I should hear Darius out before I jumped to any conclusions one way or the other. Hell, it was too late for talking. And there was only one conclusion, which was a fact: Darius had a daughter. Besides, I was all talked up and out. I didn't care if I never saw his ass again. Ever. Never would be too soon.

If I could just get through the remainder of my summer here, I was history. I knew it was a big mistake coming here. This town held too many memories, memories that haunted the deep recesses of my mind. That's why after college, I booked and never looked back. Shaneeka had attended hair school and worked in a local salon until we could make the move as roommates. Over the years, I'd visit Miss Betty, but never stayed longer than a couple of days.

Speaking of her, Miss Betty was doing great, and if I hadn't been committed to my position at the bank for the entire summer, I'd have been gone. You hear me? Gone. Shaneeka thought I was trying to run from my problems. I didn't run from problems. I handled them. I handled them efficiently and swiftly. And my solution to this problem was to dismiss Darius. Problem solved.

I hadn't told Miss Betty too much of what happened between Darius and me. She didn't need to know all that, didn't need to be all up in my business. She had remained pretty quiet about the entire situation. I just told her we had broken up, and I wouldn't be seeing him anymore. Nothing more, nothing less. Miss Betty just gave me one of her trademark looks like "Girl, you crazy. How'd you let that good catch get away?" Before she could even get wound up, I was in my bedroom, door closed and locked for good measure. I didn't want to hear it. You could play me for a fool once, but not twice. You didn't get two strikes with me.

During all of this, Darius had called me left and right for the last week. He was smart enough not to drop by the house or work. I had to give him credit—he was persistent. However, I'd take trustworthy over persistent any day. If he thought I was cold when we first met, well now, I was a winter blizzard with no signs of letting up. Some of the stuff I said to that man would have broken down some of the roughest, toughest men. I cursed his ass out backwards and forward. I called him everything but a child of God. I didn't care. Darius didn't care enough about my feelings. Damn him!

Like I said, the first week was hell two times over. But now I was working on week two and my emotions were on lockdown mode again. I was back to my old mode of operation, and it felt familiar and secure. I had only a small ache that peeked through when I least expected it. Like when I heard a certain song or saw a UPS truck or passed Applebee's, where we had our first date.

I had to give Darius credit. He was the first to effectively tear down my defenses. But never again would I let down my guard for a man. I was back to playing them before they played me. I had pretty much accepted that I would probably never marry and have children. Miss Betty had better accept it too. This week I didn't even accept calls from him. It was no use; there was no going back. I knew the facts, and Darius was not bringing me into his baby mama drama.

Tonight I was kicking it with Redman. I had run into him the other day at the drug store, at Eckerd. To make matters worse, in the midst of all this drama I was experiencing, I had severe cramps from my period and had to buy some Midol for pain. I never had cramps before, and these were the killer cramps from hell.

I heard someone calling, "Hey, baby girl. Baby girl." I looked up and there Redman was with this big smile on his face. To me, he looked like a ray of sunshine. He represented the one person I could count on to keep it real.

Redman wanted me to check out some new action flick that night, but I gave him a rain check. I remembered he was all into that fighting, karate, blowing-up-cars shit. I wasn't feeling a night out at the movies, or anything else for that matter.

So tonight was the night I was cashing it in, the rain check. I had to come back to the land of the living sooner or later. I couldn't be a walking zombie because during the day my thoughts were of Darius and at night I received no rest either because of my continuing nightmares. Something was going to have to give sooner or later. I couldn't take much more mentally, emotionally or physically.

Unfortunately, before I could step out the door to meet Redman, I had another battle to fight. A battle that was going to erupt eventually. It was destined to take place. I'd waited my whole life for this one. Waited my whole life for this one moment in time. Destiny waited.

Twenty-nine

"Mer, I hope you aren't planning on hanging out with that good-for-nothing thug tonight." Miss Betty and I were in the living room. For once, the TV was turned off.

"Miss Betty, who are you referring to as a thug?" I asked in annoyance.

"Child, don't play me for no fool. You know good and well who I'm talking about. That Redman over on Malcolm Street."

"Miss Betty, who I date and hang out with is none of your business. I'm a grown-ass woman. I don't answer to nobody but myself."

"Mer, why don't you try and make up with Darius? He was a decent man. He was good for you."

"See, you don't know what you're talking about. Darius was just like all the rest of 'em. Full of lies and bullshit. He was up to his armpits in crap. At least with Redman, I know what I'm getting."

"But, Mer, you deserve so much more. Haven't you realized that yet? You're worth so much more than you're receiving."

In utter disgust, I threw up my hands. I was bone tired, had gone back to not sleeping well and was sick of Miss Betty, my so-called mama, trying to tell me what to do. It was too late to try and play the loving mother role. All my years of pent-up anger and resentment spewed forth in a burst of hostility that surprised even me with the magnitude and force that tumbled swiftly out.

"You know what, Miss Betty? I do deserve more. I deserved so much more from you as my mother. Hell, I can't even call you mama because of your vanity. Your vanity over having a daughter. I'm a product of you and your negative environment. The apple doesn't fall too far from the tree. I'm your proof!" I screamed, hitting my chest over and over.

"Uh, no, don't go there. Don't try to blame the way your life has turned out on me. I didn't force you to make wrong choice after wrong choice. Don't bring those lies and guilt my way."

"No, for once you're going to shut up and listen. Do you really think I grew up deaf, dumb and mute? Like hear no evil, see no evil, speak no evil. Well, I saw it all. Saw all your shit. I saw all the men and women you paraded through this house. In and out. Day and night. Grandmother's house. Even though you were too busy for me. I was here. I heard, I saw, I witnessed. So don't talk to me about morals when your shit stank too."

"Girl, you'd better watch your mouth up in my house. You don't know who you talking to."

"Correction, Grandmama's house. If it wasn't for her dying and leaving this house to you, you wouldn't have shit. Nothing but a pot to piss in. And I know exactly who I'm talking to. For as long as I can remember, you've always used and abused everybody and anybody for your own personal gain. It's all about you. Always has been. And you'll use your charm, wit or body to get it.

"So if I have some atypical ideas about love and relationships, then I learned them at the feet of the master. I bow to you. I bow to you, Master," I screamed, spreading my hands out in an exaggerated motion and bowing at her feet.

"Mer, if you're going to tell it, get the story right. As you always say, don't get it twisted! Point out how Mama, your grandmother, disowned me for the first two years of your life. Put me out because I had shamed her by having a baby out of wedlock. I was a scared, homeless, naive, penniless young woman. I was only nineteen when you were born. I didn't know how I was going to survive by myself, let alone with a small baby. I could have had an abortion in somebody's back room or put you up for adoption, but I chose to have you and love you. No, we didn't have it easy growing up. Times were hard. Life was tough. We basically grew up together, but I loved you. Still do. I loved you the moment I laid eyes on you."

"Love me? Love me. You don't know the meaning of love. Criticizing and speaking harshly of my every action and move. If that's love, then I'd hate to witness your wrath towards those you hate."

"Mer, at the time, I did the best I could. I was young when I had you; I still had a lot of partying in me. Your grandmother ran her household with an iron hand. There was no room for disobedience in her home. She was the dictator, and I was the one dictated to. Growing up in a strict household, going to church every Sunday and three times during the week; when she put me out and I got a taste of freedom, I admit, I went wild. Buck wild. Yes, I craved the touch of a man, and later, women. Made me feel good, desirable and wanted. I finally had the freedom I'd always envied in others. Maybe I took it to the extreme," Miss Betty said in a stream of steady words.

"Poor, baby. Great performance. Let me give you a hand. You have a knack for switching it back to you, always about you. You know, I don't care what you say about Grandmama. You have enough sense to know you don't expose a child to various men and women coming in and out of here at all hours of the day and night. Half the time, you were so drunk that you didn't know what was going on under your very nose.

"You don't know what it was like with me being taunted and teased by my classmates because they'd heard their mother or aunt or somebody talking about you being butch, or bisexual or whatever the hell you are. I always stood out because I was your daughter. The lesbian's daughter. I was poor and the product of a single-family home just like everybody else, but the one thing that set me apart from them was you. The only friend I had from grade school to high school was Shaneeka. She was and is my one true friend. And you want to ridicule her too."

"Mer, I never knew. I never knew. You always held everything inside. At some point, you just stopped communicating with me. And, Mer, I can't change who and what I am."

"Exactly, and neither can I. I tried. I really tried with Darius, and he betrayed me and confirmed my theory. I got hurt for the first time in my life because I let Darius step inside my heart. I thought I loved a man for the first time in my life. I mean, I was really feeling him. However, I was wrong. So wrong. With Redman, I know exactly what I'm getting: good sex. That's all I want, because anything else is not even worth the effort."

"Sometimes I feel like I don't really know you. How did you get this hard, this cold?"

"Look in the mirror. Look in the goddamn mirror!"

Miss Betty just shook her head. "I pity you."

"Pity me? Don't pity me. I'm my mother's daughter. I've always, my entire life, felt like I didn't belong anywhere. Like I didn't fit in. For as long as I can remember, I've always felt unloved, unwanted and unworthy. I thought once I obtained a college degree and got out of this damn town that I would feel different, that things would be different for me. But you know what? I still don't feel. I feel like I'm still a sad, ghetto girl pretending to be something I'm not. And Miss Betty, it's too hard pretending."

"Mer, baby, I love you. I really do. I want you to be happy. What can I do to make things better? Tell me. I'll do anything."

"Love me? Love me? There's that word again. You don't love me. You never have. The only person you love is yourself. You hear me? Just yourself."

"That's not true, baby. You know that's not true. Why are you lashing out at me?"

"Yes, it is. You take and take and take. Never giving anything back. All these years, since college, I've sent you money every damn month. Never missed a month. Never once, not once have you said, 'Thank you,' or, 'You're a good daughter,' or, 'I'm proud of you.' Never."

"Mer, I've always been proud of you. Of your accomplishments."

"Umph, I couldn't tell. You wanna know what you can do for me?"

"Yes, baby, anything or I wouldn't have asked."

"Tell me. Tell me about her, about Juanita. Explain that bitch to me."

"Juanita."

"Yeah, your Juanita. I know you remember the love of your life. The mixed chick that was your heaven, sun and moon. Her shit smelled like roses to you and you worshipped the pot she pissed in. She said jump and you asked how high."

"Juanita, what does she have to do with this? That was long ago. Seems like another lifetime."

"Mama, she has everything to do with this! Can't you see that? Take off your blinders."

"I really don't want to discuss her. Like I said, that was in the past."

"No, we are going to discuss her. That's the problem. We never discussed her. She may be in your past, but she's with me every waking hour and every night when I close my eyes. Yes, even in my dreams I see her freckled face. I can't free myself from her," I said, starting to hyperventilate.

"Mer, calm down. Stop making yourself sick," she screamed, reaching for me. I shoved her away with frantic hands.

"Tell me! Tell me how a grown woman doesn't realize her female lover is molesting her own twelve-year-old daughter! Tell me that!"

"Mer, I didn't know. I swear to you, I didn't know until that day I walked in and caught . . ."

"Say it. Say it, dammit. Not speaking it out loud is not going to make it go away! You saw her with her head buried between my thighs and her fingers inside me."

"Stop, please."

"Oh, are the images too graphic? Imagine what my mind went through as a child as I was forced to put my hand down there and touch her."

"But, Mer, I beat her down to a pulp, cursed her out and threw her out of our house."

"Yeah, I give you that much credit. Even though I lived in hell for a year because of your lover, you did throw her out. And then proceeded to resent me for the rest of my life."

"How can you say that?"

"How can you not say that? You know it's true. From that point on, things changed; my world changed. Our relationship as mother and daughter shifted gears. Even as a child, I could feel it; even though I did nothing wrong, you blamed me for your breakup with your female lover. You still wanted her here and me gone."

"That's not true. Stop saying that!"

"Yes, it is true. From the time I was twelve years old, you stopped loving me! I didn't make Juanita come into my room late at night when she thought you were asleep or passed out drunk.

In fact, I tried to be as quiet as a mouse and pray that the cat wouldn't pounce. Couldn't you tell that I hated being alone with her when you'd leave at night to clean up those office buildings? Couldn't you see I hated her hugs? Now you think I'm some wild, sex-crazed woman who just looks like your daughter. But deep down, I'm still the twelve-year-old who is crying out inside because she can't understand why her own mother stopped loving her and didn't protect her from the monster."

"Mer, I didn't know you felt this way all these years. All this pent-up hostility. I'm so sorry, so very, very sorry. All these years, I'm the one who felt like I failed you as a parent. True, I always liked to have a good time. But I prided myself on showing everyone how I could do it all: raise a daughter on my own, pay the bills and still enjoy myself. When that happened with Juanita, I couldn't look at myself in the mirror because you're right, it was happening right under my nose, but I never saw it. Never saw the signs."

By now we were standing in the middle of the living room with harsh, cleansing tears streaming down our faces. Neither one of us made an attempt to wipe them away. We looked at each other. Seeing through the masks. Really seeing the people we were with all our insecurities. Secrets, deep feelings finally revealed. Hands balled into tight fists. Wondering what's next. What do we do now? Where do we go from here?

I don't know who made the first move, took the first step. All I know is that I felt Miss Betty's, my mama's arms, around me for the first time in a long time and it felt so right, so good. I hesitated for only a moment before I wrapped my arms around Miss Betty and held on for dear life. I wanted to hold on to that feeling and never let it go. We both spoke at the same time, interrupting each other, both crying rivers of tears, murmuring promises to each other as I felt brick walls crumbling down. Walls that had been up for years, built out of pain and tragedy. Each brick that fell gave me back a piece of myself.

Later, Miss Betty made a big pot of black coffee, and we sat down at the kitchen table and talked. Cried some more. Talked almost everything out. Said most of it, cleared the air. Didn't hold anything back. It was impossible to release all our unspoken words, thoughts in one night. However, there would be many nights of talking.

We talked into the wee hours of the morning. Held hands. Looked eye to eye. Talked until the sun meekly peeked over the horizon and showed signs of a wonderful new beginning in the form of another day. I exposed and expressed emotions that had been buried so deeply within; truths came out that I didn't even realize I was harboring.

Mama explained to me how she felt when my daddy died and when my grandmother disowned her and wouldn't provide any source of financial support. She felt lost and abandoned. Mama described how she had never felt so alone in the world as she had back then. Yet she made a vow to herself and God that somehow she'd make a way for her baby daughter. Like I said, that was a night of true revelations that brought forth a means for forgiveness and healing. I felt the gates bursting open.

Thirty

Redman and I never hooked up that night, the night of revelations and truths. We finally got together the following Saturday. We planned to hang out all day and have a cookout at a state park. Adams Park was a local hangout that was a great place for family reunions, picnics and pickup basketball games. It housed a small man-made lake, picnic tables, a few worn-out barbeque grills, two playgrounds for the kids and nature and bike and walking trails. By this time, it was two weeks after the Darius and his mother "spilling the beans incident." Darius was still calling, but his calls were gradually tapering off. Miss Betty, at my request, always informed him that I was unavailable.

So it was a hot and muggy Saturday afternoon when Redman and I headed over to Piggly Wiggly to pick up some food and supplies for our cookout. We had gotten a late start and hadn't really planned out in advance what we'd need in the way of food to grill. I had on a tight-fitting red short set with some cute strappy sandals and an ankle bracelet. Typical hoochie wear. With my braids pulled back and secured with a large black scrunchie, I was looking kind of cute, if I may say so myself. I was finally getting back to my old self without big bags under my eyes and walking around depressed all day. With his denim baggy shorts, Atlanta Braves jersey and baseball cap on backwards, Redman was looking good too. Sometimes I thought he was such a waste to society because he was an intelligent, good-looking, sexy brother who could have done almost anything with his life, yet he chose to do absolutely nothing. Most people looked upon him as a menace to society. In my opinion, it still wasn't too late.

The plan was that Redman and I would split up the short grocery list, that I'd just scribbled down, which consisted of about twelve items, and meet back at the checkout counter to speed up our shopping process. We wanted to have the grill up and smoking by one o'clock. I hadn't had any barbeque all summer and was looking forward to sinking my teeth into some. Baby-back ribs, chopped barbeque and barbeque chicken were calling my name. I was over in the aisle that displayed charcoal, matches and picnic stuff when I thought I felt someone staring at me. I could feel the tiny hairs rising on my neck and arms. I quickly dismissed the feeling and continued to comparison shop, but soon couldn't resist the urge to look up from my examination of the various lighter fluids.

When I looked up and turned slightly to my right, I stared straight into the handsome face of Darius.

For a brief second, I realized how much I had missed him in my life. Wanted to run into his strong arms. Feel him whisper that everything would be okay. Hear him say out loud that we'd survive this; we'd make it work. Feel him moving around inside me like he belonged there. Unfortunately, this lasted just a few seconds. Anger, hurt and betrayal soon replaced it.

Darius wasn't looking that well. He had on wrinkled blue jeans that had seen better days, a faded gray wife beater T-shirt and a day-old beard graced his face. He had definitely seen better days. Much better.

Before I broke the silent trance, we intensely locked eyes for a few seconds. Our eyes spoke where words weren't possible. Our eyes spoke of love, longing and the pain of separation. I felt my heart kinda lurch forward, and my eyes started to water. In the next instance, my eyes revealed the hurt of betrayal. I turned quickly away before my emotions got the best of me.

"Mercedes, can I talk to you for a moment?" he asked, slowly walking in my direction with outstretched hands. He held them up as if calling a truce.

"No, Darius, I think I've made it perfectly clear that I don't want to have anything else to do with you. I have nothing more to say to you." Dabbing at the corner of my eyes with my finger, I didn't even turn around. I pretended to look at the lighter fluid.

"Mer, just let me explain. Then you don't ever have to see me or talk to me again, please," he said, a whining in his trembling voice. I'd never seen this side of him before. Darius looked and sounded like a lost child who had been separated from his mother.

For a moment, just a brief moment, when I turned and looked at him, I truly wanted to listen to what he had to say. Wanted to hear his side of things. Absorb it all. I wanted to hear what he had to say so that everything would be okay again. We could go back to the way we were when we were happy. However, I couldn't chance opening my heart again to Darius that way. Not now. Not ever.

Instead I rudely said, "No. I'm not interested in whatever you have to say. Can't you understand that? I don't care what you have to say. It doesn't matter. Just go back to your wife and child. Have a happy freaking life and forget I ever existed, as I have with you."

That comment hit him hard because I sensed the change in his stance and demeanor.

"Mer, please. Don't make me beg," he said, reaching for my elbow.

"Don't then. It doesn't become you."

Redman took that moment to make an appearance at my side. I'm glad he did, because just the touch of Darius's hand made me momentarily weak in the knees and other places. I felt my broken heart lurch forward yet again.

"I think you heard the lady. Take your hands off her," Redman said, magically appearing at my side looking like a thugged-out version of a gallant black knight.

Darius looked from me to Redman and then back to me with unspoken questions in his face. I saw the hurt in his eyes immediately. I knew he thought I was fucking Redman, and Darius was right: I couldn't wait to get some. I knew Darius had laid it on his ex, just for old time's sake. Wouldn't put it past him. His precious first love.

"I think the lady can speak for herself," he said, pushing out his chest for emphasis and taking a fighting stance.

"No, bro. I'm speaking for her today. And this is the last time saying it nicely, brotha. Back down. Mer doesn't want your tired ass. Accept it like a man and move on."

Darius didn't back down as he and Redman sized each other up. If a fight broke out in the middle of Piggly Wiggly, I couldn't say who would win. Darius had the height and body weight, but Redman had street smarts and could handle his own too.

"You stay out of this, man! This is none of your damn business. Mercedes," Darius screamed, holding up his hands. "Talk to me. Say something. Anything."

"Darius, just go, okay? It was over before it began. There's nothing more to say."

"Oh, it's like that? You'll give up on us that easily? Our time together meant nothing to you? How could I have ever thought your ass was special?"

I wanted to scream for the entire store to hear that our time together had been special and I'd never forget this summer. I longed to get on the store intercom and make that announcement to anyone who would listen. Instead, I foolishly stated the opposite.

"Yeah, as far as I'm concerned, there is no us. Never was. You were just a good time. Someone to pass the summer with. You messed the fuck up. So be gone," I said as Redman put his arm around my waist, leading me to the checkout.

As much as I wanted to, I didn't dare look back. As I held my breath, I looked straight ahead, at nothing. Put one foot in front of the other. I could feel the aura of defeat and disappointment that surrounded Darius as he watched us walk off. Walk off like a couple that had shared intimacies.

Redman was laughing. "Mercedes, you must have put it on him good. Had the nigga begging to come back. That's power, baby. That's power." Even though I laughed, somewhere deep inside, I didn't think that shit was funny.

Thirty-one

Darius slowly and defeatedly walked up to the express checkout at the checkout lane next to us. We were only a few feet apart, yet the distance seemed like miles. This time he didn't even look in my direction. I could feel the space between us growing wider and wider. Made me feel like I was invisible and worthless. For good measure, Redman glanced over at him with a smirk on his full lips, caressed my ass with his hand and pulled me closer as he kissed my forehead. I smiled up at him as if all was perfect in my world. I had the world on my shoulders; I was the queen bee and all was freaking perfect.

Even though I don't remember much of the fifteen-minute drive over, Redman and I arrived at the park. After finally securing a space to set up, he threw down on the ribs and the chicken, but I still wasn't feeling it. My good mood had gone straight to hell in a handbasket. Though there was plenty of beer, that didn't even give me my usual mellow buzz. As we basked in the afternoon sun, I pretended to have a good time. I kept thinking about how defeated Darius looked in the grocery store checkout line. Maybe Mama—I was calling Miss Betty Mama by now—and Shaneeka were right; maybe I needed to at least hear him out. See what he had to say. I couldn't get that final image of Darius off my mind. That was the least I could do. Hear him out. Get closure. Closure was a good thing.

By the time Redman and I left Adam's Park that evening, the sun was making its final appearance for the day as it barely peeked over the horizon, and families were pretty much packing up and heading home after a fun-filled day. I was probably two shades darker. After Redman stroked my braids and massaged my shoulders to ease my tension, I had fallen asleep on our large purple beach towel and soaked up the summer sun. I woke to Redman stroking me through my thin top, and I realized I was still totally stuffed from all the food and beer.

It was a lazy, hot day, typical in south Georgia during the late summer. I had a lot on my mind, but Redman didn't pry. I caught him staring at me a few times, but I guess he figured if I wanted to talk, I would. I was thankful that he didn't ask a lot of questions about me and Darius. Eventually I started to talk. I needed release. I wanted to get another man's opinion and point of view. I told Redman a little about my situation, and believe it or not, he thought I should talk to Darius too. That shocked me. I just knew he was going to say that I was doing the right thing by letting go.

"Talk to the man."

"Why?"

"Mer, if the man was willing to beg like a little punk, then he's seriously feeling you."

"I don't know."

"What's there to know? I know it's killing you to find out the details. Talk to him."

"But he lied to me."

"No, he didn't lie; he just didn't tell you the whole story. There's a difference. Probably thought you couldn't handle the truth. And he was right."

"Umph."

"Baby girl, you know I'm right. You repress and internalize too much shit."

"Oh, so now you're my shrink?"

"Just call me Dr. Redman."

"Yeah, whatever."

"I'm just saying, sometimes you have to release your past to secure your future."

"What is that shit suppose to mean?"

"All I'm saying is that you need to let go some of that baggage from your past. Forgiveness works wonders, boo."

"Yeah?"

"Forgiveness might open up a world of possibilities for you."

"That's some deep shit," I said, absorbing the knowledge that Redman had dropped on me.

"I can be a deep brother."

"Yeah, you can. I'll think about what you said."

"Bet. Can't ask for more than that."

As we were packing up our personal items, throwing away trash and heading back to the car, Redman asked if I was going to crash at his apartment for a while.

"Sure. You're not trying to get rid of me yet, are you?" Redman never ceased to amaze me. One minute he could be deep and the next he was trying to get some. I know what people thought they were getting when they looked at him from outward appearances, but inside, he was so much more.

"Not you, Mer. Not you."

"You better not." I flashed a smile that didn't quite make it to my face or eyes.

I knew what he had on his mind because I had the same on mine. I hadn't had any in a while and I was horny as hell. Maybe getting some would make me feel better and lift my pissy mood.

Before the night was over, after drinking some more cheap wine and smoking some blunts, we were embraced in the throes of screwing; I say screwing because I now knew what it felt like to make love.

Redman had one of the thickest and prettiest dicks I had ever seen on a man. You'd never suspect it with his wiry frame, but he did. I remember the first time he pulled down his drawers and I saw it, almost scared the heebie-jeebies out of me. That fear soon dissipated when I climbed on that big boy and rode it like there was no tomorrow. I loved to do that shit, just ride big boy until he couldn't handle any more.

Tonight, however, somehow, even though it felt good, it wasn't the same. There just wasn't an emotional connection. We were going through the motions, but it wasn't the same. My body was definitely enjoying it, but my mind was elsewhere. Far, far away. My bag of tricks wasn't even opened and that was too bad since I'd spent good money at Inserection at the beginning of the summer. Don't get me wrong. I moaned and came twice from Redman just using his tongue to go in and out while I kneeled above his face on the bed. When he inserted two fingers inside and played with my clit with his thumb, that took me over the top. Yeah, took the edge off my problems.

Around midnight, I pulled myself from Redman's long legs that were entangled over mine, redressed and headed to my car as a police cruiser passed slowly by. They were forever cruising this neighborhood. Zone Four was one of the toughest beats. There was the usual gang and drug activity and prostitution taking place. Out of the corner of my eye, I saw the black police officers checking me out. Been there, done that.

For a hot second, I flashed back to these two police officers, partners, that did me a while ago. We exchanged sex for a traffic ticket. Actually, I initiated the swap. I couldn't handle another ticket on my record. Hell, my insurance was already high enough, and more points would do me in. I always thought there was just something sexy about men in uniform. Turned me the hell on. That night that shit was off the hook. Doing a police officer was one of my fantasies; two was even better.

They came over to my apartment dressed in their police uniforms and guns, role-played, used their handcuffs, and pleased every nook and cranny of my body. I got the shivers just thinking about it now. They were into domination; I had to do anything they told me to do, and believe me, they were both inventive and creative in their requests. They played good cop, bad cop. Played it well too. The good cop granted all my deepest desires, and there were many. If I was bad, then the bad cop got to punish me. Sweet pain. Bad cop would spank my ass and the good cop would kiss it where it hurt. We went at it until the wee hours of the morning. Now, every time I saw police officers, I had flashbacks. However . . . I quickly dismissed that image. As I walked out of Redman's, I realized that I was changing. For the better.

Thirty-two

After my date with Redman, I knew it would be a while before I saw him again. We were like that. We could go long periods of time without any physical or verbal contact. We enjoyed each other because there were no commitments between us. We made each other feel good at that moment in time and then went our separate ways, back to our separate, different lives. By Monday, he'd probably have someone else in his bed. And I didn't care. I also realized that I wasn't in a hurry to be with him again, sexually, anyway.

I also made the final decision not to talk with Darius. I had messed things up in the grocery store, and besides, I was too selfish to share him with an ex and a daughter. I was never one for all that baby mama drama. Not this one. I didn't have to put up with that shit. Too much baggage.

There was always a plan B. My plan for the remainder of my stay, which had been extended by the bank manager, was to immerse myself in my job. Who knew? Maybe I would be such a productive and efficient worker that I'd be named Employee of the Month. Yipeee! Not. So that's exactly what I did. I was early to work and left late. I helped out with the other reps' workloads whenever possible. By the time Mama and I sat down to dinner in the evenings, washed the dishes together, talked, all I could think about was sleep. Oh yeah, my nightmares were gone. Cleaning out my closet, of all the skeletons, did wonders. So ironically, sleep was now my escape and salvation. I craved it.

Mama and I had come far, yet I realized that we still had a long way to go. Regardless of our revelations, Mama was still a hard lady to live with. She was opinionated, stubborn and bullheaded. I guess that wasn't going to change overnight, if ever. Probably never. We were learning to agree to disagree.

Shaneeka and her new boyfriend, they were still kicking it. They surprised me one weekend by driving down and taking me out to dinner at Outback Steakhouse. We even drove out to visit her family. Shaneeka looked good, peaceful even. Had a radiant glow about her. We had a really wonderful time; took my mind off the fact that I was just surviving day by day. I guess it's true what they say about opposites attract. Shaneeka was still ghetto fabulous and the new guy, Chris, was Mr. Conservative. They seemed happy, so who was I to judge?

This Monday afternoon found me doing some follow-up work and much-needed filing at my desk. Darius no longer attempted to call me at home or at work, and every time a UPS driver came through our branch, my heartbeat would momentarily speed up until I realized that the driver wasn't him. As much as I knew it was over, I still craved to see him just one more time. Just to place my finger in his dimple and see that gorgeous smile light up his entire face. Just to see him and know he wasn't a figment of my imagination.

I was daydreaming, which was something I was doing a lot of lately, and thinking about going with Mama out to the local mall to pick out something for her to wear on her date. Since her operation, she had lost some weight. Her womanly figure had needed to lose a few pounds, and if I may say so myself, once she got her hair colored and freshly permed, nails done, my mama was all that and then some. She reminded me of an older version of the comedian Monique.

Evidently, Mr. Peterson, our neighbor a few doors down, thought so too. I had noticed recently, he was always around the house fixing this or that, Mr. Handyman himself. The other night, he finally coughed up the courage to ask her out to the movies. I was shocked that Mama asked me to go with her to pick out some new clothes to accommodate her weight loss. Secretly, I was pleased. We had never really done mother-daughter stuff together. We made a day of it. We got an early start on a Saturday morning. We shopped, ate lunch, shopped some more and generally just hung out.

I was so into my daydream and paperwork that I didn't notice the thirty-something woman quietly sit down in the chair in front of my desk with a young child sound asleep on her lap. I didn't notice until she gently cleared her throat. I looked up and immediately knew. I knew. It was obvious that the woman sitting before me was once beautiful with her delicate bone structure, high cheekbones and large doelike eyes.

However, you could tell that she had seen some hard times. It showed in her dull eyes and the small lines that ran crisscross around her mouth and eyes. She was petite, dainty and carried an air of uncertainty. This woman came across as someone who needed pampering and careful handling. With her short-cropped hair that framed her face, she also had these huge, expressive eyes that scanned my face in search of discovery and recognition.

The young girl that sat in her lap was absolutely beautiful. In sleep, she looked like an angel with her long eyelashes, brown skin and pouted lips. Her long braids were perfectly tied in place with blue ribbons. And on her left cheek was a dimple. A familiar dimple.

"Hi, Miss Jackson. I'm Latrice Dargon, Darius's ex-wife," she said hesitantly, clearing her throat again and offering her fragile hand for a handshake. Her hand was weak and thin, as if she didn't have the strength to offer a firm grip.

I looked at her like I'd seen the ghost from Christmas past.

"Listen, I know this is a shock, but before you say anything, please hear me out. Could we go somewhere and talk? I promise, I won't take up much of your time."

I still hadn't said anything, just nodded my head and stiffly stood up from my desk. Thankfully, Latrice took that as a yes and followed distantly and hesitantly behind me. I could feel her eyes taking me in inch by inch. I somehow managed to murmur to a teller that I was going on break. I led Latrice to an empty conference room in back that we used to make personal phone calls, and closed the door to offer us some privacy. I breathed in and out to steady myself and then turned to face her. I don't know who was more afraid. I could tell from the expression on her face that this was not easy for her.

"Did Darius send you here?"

"No, Mercedes, he didn't. I'm sorry. May I call you Mercedes?"

I nodded my head. I really wanted to ask her what the hell she wanted.

I threw up my hands. "How may I help you? Why are you here?"

Latrice shifted the weight of her daughter—their daughter—and settled into the closest chair. I remained standing. I figured I'd have the upper hand if I towered above her. I wasn't ready to face her eye to eye.

"Mostly I came out of curiosity."

"I don't follow."

"I wanted to see the lady who stole Darius's heart from me."

"I haven't stolen anything. Darius and I are no longer together. Anyway, I think crack stole that away."

I saw her wince at my words.

"Actually, you're wrong. You may not be there physically, but you're definitely there. In his heart. Believe me. I'm a woman, was once his woman, and I know."

"So why are you telling me this? Again, why are you even here? What do you want from me?"

Latrice shifted positions again. Scooted her daughter, their daughter, up higher into the cradle of her thin arms.

"I'm sure Darius told you a few things about me. Most not flattering. Well, I cleaned up my act, and I admit, I came back to claim my man. My first love. A good man."

"Um. You had a funny way of showing it."

"It's funny how the grass always looks greener on the other side. However, once you get a closer inspection, you see that the grass could use a serious trim and has a bunch of weeds growing all over the place."

I chose to remain silent and looked down at my fingernails. It was definitely time for a fill-in. Maybe I'd get a French manicure next time.

"To be honest, I didn't care who was in the picture. I made a lot of mistakes, but now I am clean and wanted to reclaim what I lost."

"What did you lose?"

"I lost a precious jewel in Darius. Like I said before, the grass always looked greener on the other side, the wrong side. Darius was stable, hardworking and a family man. I had dated him since we were teenagers; he was all I knew. So even though he was good to me, to us, I thought I was missing something, and I set out to find out what that was. I started hanging out when he would leave for work. Would leave the baby with a sitter for hours."

I still didn't respond, I sat down across from her with my hands palms down on the massive conference room table.

"Bottom line, I got in over my head, hung with the wrong crew and had an affair. Darius caught us in our own bed, and of course that hurt Darius dearly. To the core.

"Yet Darius still stood by my side when he found out I had a serious drug problem; I just wasn't ready to help myself. I had to learn the hard way. I was hardheaded. I laughed in his face and called him all sorts of names, even lied and told him his own daughter wasn't his. Another low blow, because this child here is his heart."

"Listen, I don't want to hear this. You shouldn't be telling me this, because there's nothing I can do about your situation or his. I'll show you out."

"Please hear me out. This is very hard for me. I came back to claim him, and he doesn't want me anymore. And I had to see the woman who took him away from me after he promised, on his life, that he'd always love only me. You see, Darius loves deeply and hard. He gives everything he has. There is no middle ground with him."

"Well, you can have him; I'm leaving soon. Going back to Atlanta. This isn't my problem."

Latrice threw up her hands to silence me like she hadn't heard a word I said. "Please talk to him. Please. He's a good man, and I didn't mean to bring any more trouble or pain his way. You see, I don't want to hurt him again. He was unhappy for so long because of me."

"I don't know. I don't need this right now. I've moved on."

"Have you? Please just talk to him, that's all. Just talk."

Latrice started to stand up, her daughter woke up and looked straight at me with those big black eyes.

I smiled and she smiled back shyly. I saw Darius all over her adorable face. Like he spit her out. I could see how she was his heart.

"Talk to him." Latrice said, grabbing my hand and squeezing gently. "Believe me, this was not easy for me . . . to confront you this way. But I know Darius, have known him my entire life. You got the man sprung. He needs you. Desperately."

"I . . ."

She held up her free hand to shush me. "I'm here only for a few more days to straighten out some business, get visitation issues resolved and then I'm gone. I have to reclaim my life and make amends with a lot of people. I know I'm not wanted here any longer, because I don't own Darius's heart anymore.

"You do," she said, releasing my hand. "I envy you. Be happy."

"Thank you," was all I managed to murmur. For some reason, I felt like crying like a baby.

"Mommy, who's that?"

"Just a very special woman who will make your daddy happy again."

"Daddy's not happy?"

"He will be. Soon." Latrice looked back at me and nodded. "Very soon."

Latrice and her daughter quietly let themselves out. I laid my head on the cold conference room table, attempted to compose myself and cried silent, fresh tears. It seemed like lately, I'd cried enough tears to last a lifetime.

Thirty-three

After careful consideration and lots of tossing and turning, I decided to meet and talk with Darius. Just talk. Find out why. My time in small-town America was quickly coming to an end, and I knew I couldn't go home without knowing the details. The who, what, when, where, why and how. This was eating me up inside. Everybody—Mama, Shaneeka, even Redman—said I should talk to the man. Before I lost my nerve, I showed up at Darius's house one humid evening after work. Unannounced.

I had worked overtime again and was on my way home. Before I knew what I was doing, I turned my car around at the four-way stop and found myself driving in the opposite direction. On the way over, my mind was spinning and dipping all over the place. I didn't know what I'd say or do. I didn't know what Darius would say or do. I had no idea how this drama would play out.

When I pulled up into Darius's driveway, I didn't see his mom's car. That was good; she wasn't home, and I wouldn't have to face her too. I still hadn't figured her out yet. I'd deal with her at another place and time.

However, I saw Darius's black truck pulled over to the side of the house, near a water hose. It looked like he had recently washed his truck, because I saw cleaning supplies scattered on the grass along with some old rags. I knew he was there, and my heartbeat sped up. I looked down at my hands, and they were shaking to an unknown hip-hop beat. I sat in my car for a few minutes just trying to get up my nerve and compose myself. I'd start to open the car door, get out, and then lose my nerve. I'd take a few breaths and start again. I repeated this process several times.

This was so unlike me; I wasn't afraid of a man. I'd go toe-to-toe with any man, any day. Shit, I grew up in the projects. I didn't back down from situations. Fighting was an every day part of life if you wanted to survive. I'd had my share of wins and losses against males and females. In the end, even if a man beat my ass, I'd at least stepped to him and held my own.

My nervousness alone let me know that Darius was indeed different. Something special. There were a few times that I almost cranked up my car and simply drove off, just left. Finally after about twenty minutes, after realizing how ridiculous I was behaving, I opened my car door and quickly stepped out before I lost my nerve again. I ran up the sidewalk to the door directly off the basement. Even though it hadn't been that long, everything felt different, as if it had been forever since I'd been this way. As if it had all been a dream.

I definitely didn't know what to expect behind that door. Hell, I didn't even know if he'd let me in or slam the door in my face as he laughed hysterically while I stumbled down the walkway to my waiting car in utter embarrassment and shame. However, there was no turning back now. I had to do this. For myself. For some peace. I took two deep breaths and knocked two hard knocks on the door; I didn't see a doorbell.

Then I just stood there holding my breath. At first, I didn't hear any sounds from within. And on the outside, everything seemed to stand still. The birds ceased to chirp in the trees, flowing traffic stood still and the music that was blasting, earlier, from next door, miraculously disappeared. My forehead broke out in small sweat beads that I wiped off with the back of my right hand. I realized my palms were sweaty. I bit down on my lower lip.

There. I heard sounds of movement coming from inside. Faint sounds. Heavy footsteps heading in my direction. Coming closer. I braced myself. Almost there. I forced my face to hold a confident, I'm every woman, noncombative smile in place. Then it happened. The door flung open, and I was face-to-face with Darius for the first time in weeks.

Instantly I was assaulted with all kinds of emotions, and my five senses took over. I smelled a musky, masculine, woodsy scent seeping from his pours. My eyes took in his dimple, and I stopped myself from sticking my finger in it. My eyes were blinded by his ruggedness. My body and mind went into meltdown.

I blinked and opened my mouth to speak, but nothing came out. Not a sound. I tried to swallow, but my throat was dry. I needed some water. So I just stood there looking as humble as possible. Hoping he could read my mind.

On closer inspection, Darius's face showed no emotions at all. Not even a smile. I didn't see love or hate or any emotion. His expression remained neutral, and that worried me. Maybe this was a mistake. He spoke first, and for the first time, I saw anger. Even though it was expected, it still threw me for a loop. Made me feel weaker. Unsure of myself.

"What do you want?" he asked harshly.

"I . . . I wanted to talk with you for a minute," I answered as humbly as possible.

"Oh, you want to talk now?" he asked, laughing as if I had told a humorous joke on *Comic View*. "She wants to talk," he announced into the air.

"Yes, if that's okay," I said, near whispering.

"You didn't want to talk when I wanted to. Well, I'm busy right now."

"I'm sorry. I should have called first."

"Yeah, you should have."

There was an awkward moment of silence. I looked down at the sidewalk, while Darius's eyes never left my face. I could feel him scoping me out.

"Listen, I don't want to inconvience you. Maybe we could do this another time?"

"No, no, come on in. Let's get this over with," he said, turning to go back inside. "You have five minutes. No more, no less. Talk," he commanded with his back to me.

"You're not making this easy."

"Well, life isn't easy. Did you make it easy for me?"

"I guess not."

"Mercedes, what do you want? Spit it out. You're not one for holding back. Talk to me. I don't have all day. I have important things to do."

Again, my throat went dry and I couldn't say anything.

"Oh, let me guess. I know what you want. You came by for me to fuck you, right? I know how you're into no-commitment fucking."

After realizing he wasn't joking, I just stared in utter disbelief.

"Darius, it's not even . . ." I started to say, but he abruptly cut me off.

"Well, you're in luck. You were such a good lay, and since I desire no commitment from you either, I'll do you."

With that, Darius snatched me by the back of my braids and forced his lips onto mine as he kicked his front door closed with his right foot. As I let out a startled cry, his hot tongue went into my mouth without any gentleness. Foreplay wasn't on his agenda today. Gentleness had left the building.

Thirty-four

Darius kissed me harshly, and his hands roamed all over my body. Reclaiming it. By now I was kicking and struggling to get away from his ever-present hands. Darius wouldn't let loose or give me any slack. I heard a ripping sound and quickly realized my skirt and blouse were literally being torn off. We were up against a corner wall, knocked a photo down, and Darius was still clawing at my black skirt. Simultaneously, he managed to pull my skirt up and my panties down to my ankles as he restrained my hands. I heard his zipper being unzipped.

In the next few seconds, everything happened in slow motion. He turned me around so that I was facing the wall. Actually had my face smashed into the wall. Darius expertly had my blouse off and discarded as he groped and squeezed at my breasts. When he plunged into me from behind, I gasped for breath. Even though I was crying, Darius held me against the wall by both wrists as he went in and out, showing me no mercy.

"Stop crying, Mer. Don't you like a little pain? I thought you liked a little S and M? Gets you off. Takes you over the top, over the edge."

"Darius, *stop!* This is not you!"

"Hell, you don't know what's me; never took the time to find out. Now, work with me, baby. I'm giving you what you like."

"*No!* Not like this."

"Don't worry; after we're finished, you can go, because I have places to go and people to see."

Darius proceeded to fuck the living daylights out of me and whisper obscenities in my ear. He called me every nasty, degrading name he could think of. All the while, he was inside me, plunging away at a frantic pace. Showed my ass not an ounce of mercy. His teeth bit into my neck and his free hand was pinching my nipples between his fingers as I grimaced in pain.

When I wouldn't perform as he wanted me to, he slapped my ass a couple of times to get me going. My head was banging upside the wall as he went in and out at an urgent pace. Darius would spank me with one hand as his other hand firmly encircled my neck.

Slap. Slap. "Like that, don't you?" If I didn't answer, he slapped my ass again, harder. I could feel my ass cheeks stinging and bruising from his blows. By now, I was crying, because he had hurt my feelings, and at the same time, amazingly, I was enjoying it. As Darius sensed I was getting into this assault, his words become harsher, as did his thrusts and slaps. Right as I felt him about to explode, he shifted me around by my wrists onto my knees. Then he squirted all into my face. His face held a strange mixture of pleasure and disgust.

Darius then proceeded to grab my clothes up from the floor and throw them at me. "Get dressed and get out. You got what you came for. So now be gone. No strings attached."

I didn't say anything. I couldn't believe what had just happened. How could he treat me like trash?

"If you like that shit that way, Mercedes, you got some serious issues. That's totally fucked up. Somebody seriously fucked up your head. You were seriously into that. Please, for your sake, seek therapy. Fast."

"I need to explain . . ." I murmured, looking up at him with his juices all over my face.

"I don't want to hear it. I finally realize I don't want you. You don't even value your own worth, and if you can't, then why should I? You don't even know what a woman's worth is all about. And guess what? As a man, I can't tell you. A woman's worth, that's something you have to know and desire for yourself."

By now, I was dressing quickly, hiding myself from his view and sobbing quietly as I searched for my keys and purse.

"Mercedes, get dressed and get out. You got what you wanted. And I don't need you, because I don't have a problem finding women to fuck in this town. I'm looking for the special lady I can make love to. I'm gonna find me somebody who's not afraid to let go and see where love takes them. If I need a booty call before you leave town, I'll call you up."

"Darius, please," I whined, trying to smooth down my braids, which were all over the place. "Listen to me for a minute."

"Have a good life, Mer. Maybe I'll see you around," he said calmly as he started to walk away, leaving me behind like I was the discarded trash of the day. "I need to take a shower. Suddenly I feel dirty. Let yourself out."

Thirty-five

"Girl, no, he didn't say that shit to you!" Shaneeka shrieked into the phone. Before she burst my eardrum, I held the phone away from my right ear.

"Yes, he did. He said I didn't value my own worth."

"Well, Darius needs to return that shit back where he bought it. Girl, there are more fish in the sea than Darius."

I remained silent as I picked at a hangnail and cradled the phone between my ear and shoulder. My thoughts wandered.

"Hello? Mer?"

"I'm here. Just thinking about stuff."

"Like what?"

"Maybe Darius is right. Miss Betty—I mean Mama—and I have had our share of ups and downs over the years. And you know what that stems from. Old hurts are hard to heal. Thankfully, Mama and I are working on our differences. You know, at least we are communicating. That's a good start."

"Mer, that's good to hear about you and Miss Betty. But Darius, well, Mer, he didn't have to be so cold-blooded with it. He's not your damn shrink."

I sighed. "I know, but his point came across loud and clear. Got me to thinking. About my life."

"Let it go, girl. We all have our inner demons to deal with."

"Unfortunately, I haven't been dealing with mine."

"You're on the right path now. Anyway, you have to deal with that town for only a few more weeks and then you are out of there."

"I know. I'm counting down the weeks and days."

"I hear you."

"Pretty soon I'm going to start counting down the hours."

"Girl, we are going to really hang out once you hit town. Put you back in a good mood. Have a screw-Darius party. So get ready to party your blues away!"

"I'm looking forward to it; I haven't been in a club in so long I wouldn't know how to act."

"Listen, maybe I'll get Chris to hook you up with one of his friends."

"Uh, no thanks."

"Why, girl?"

"I don't think any of Chris's friends would be my type. And besides, I don't have any problems meeting men."

"Well, you know what?"

"What? Because I know you're going to tell me."

"I used to think the same thing. Sometimes you have to think outside the box. At first I didn't think Chris was my type, but look at us now. We are tighter than glue, and he makes me happy. I've even trained him in the bedroom. Knows what makes mommy meow like a kitten."

"Well, I'm happy for you, girl, but I'm going to chill for a while. You feel me?"

"Not 'Miss I got to have some dick' Jackson?"

We both broke up in laughter at that.

"Not the chick who uses sex like others use a cigarette or alcohol."

I laughed again because I couldn't believe it my damn self.

"Yes. Believe it or not, you know, things change; I need to put my life in order."

"Well, you know I'm with you one hundred percent, girl. I used to be worried about you sometimes."

"I know, and thanks."

"Thanks for what?"

"For being my friend through thick and thin, for always being here for me. For being here for me during my lowest moments."

"Girl, you know I love you. Always have and always will. Since that first day I saw you in first grade."

"Me, too. I wouldn't trade you for a million dollars."

"Shit, you better hope I don't have to make that choice. For a million dollars, I'd be like, 'Mercedes who?' "

We both fell out, once again, in laughter. It felt good to laugh for a change. For a minute, I thought I had forgotten how.

Silence set in.

"I have to give it to Darius though."

"Why?"

"Girl, Darius almost made you love him."

I hesitated. "Everybody knows, almost doesn't count."

"I guess you're right."

"Listen, I've got to get off this phone because Chris is coming by soon, but I got to tell you this."

"Tell me what?"

"Mer, Jamal had the nerve to call me again the other day and wanted to come over. Said he had been doing a lot of thinking and realized what a special lady he had in me."

"No, girl, you kidding. What did you say to that fool?"

"I wish I was kidding, girl. I told him, 'Too little too late.' I informed him I had found a real man, both in bed and out, and then I calmly hung up the phone. Talk about liberating."

"Good for you. Good for you, girl. You don't need that back in your life."

"And you know it."

"So he got over us thrashing his place?"

"Girl, please. Jamal's drug money had that mess fixed up and repaired by the end of the week."

"True."

"He said my actions proved how much I loved him."

"What did you say?"

"That's when I hung up the phone."

"Good for you!"

"Oops, there's the doorbell. Tell Miss Betty hello for me and call me if you need me. You'll be all right, girl. God don't like ugly and what Darius did was ugly."

"I know. I will. Bye."

"Bye, girl."

After hanging up the phone, I felt much better. I just needed to confide in someone who wouldn't judge me or bullshit me, and to be honest, I didn't have many names in my phone book that I could call. It had been a couple of days since the encounter with Darius. Long days. At first I was pissed beyond pisstivity, but I'd had a lot of time to think about what went down. Even though Darius was wrong in his actions, some of the stuff he said was true. Too true. It hit home.

Yeah, I'd had a couple of days to calm down. When I first arrived home after he threw me out, I went flat-out ballistic. Luckily Mama was out. I went straight to my room and slammed the door so hard that the thin walls rattled. I hadn't shed a tear since I left him and didn't intend to. But then, I looked in the mirror and lost it. When I saw the hurt and fear in my eyes, I totally lost it.

There was even a bruise around my neck from him holding me so tightly.

Such an internal rage overcame me that I thought I had lost my freaking mind. As I stared at my reflection, a sense of total disgust encircled and engulfed me. Much like that day in the shower, my entire body started to shake and tremble. I broke out in a cold sweat, and I felt the walls closing in on me. Moving closer and closer. The tears came fast and hard, and I wanted to hurt somebody, hurt myself.

At that moment, I hated who I was, who I had become. As cleansing tears streamed down my face, I tore my old room up. How dare he say those hateful things to me? Darius didn't know me. Didn't know what I had been through. Hadn't walked in my shoes. I started screaming and cursing and totally trashing my bedroom. I was out of control in a major way. As never before.

Anything my hands came in touch with was destroyed within seconds. Photos were shredded; my bedspread and pillows were tossed; everything was knocked off my oak dresser to the floor; clothes were flying left and right from my closet. Nothing was safe. By the time I finally collapsed, balled up by a corner wall, I was all cried out. I spent the next few minutes rocking back and forth. Back and forth. Arms hugging myself. By the time Mama made it back, I was composed and everything was back in order as if it had never happened. In my mind, it never did. Darius never happened.

The past couple of days I went to work, came straight home and hung out in my room and took a mental inventory of my life. What I saw wasn't cute. Unfortunately, the face in the mirror that had done much dirt was mine. Darius was right. I'd made many bad choices in my lifetime. Some of my choices were destructive and downright degrading and disrespectful to myself as a woman.

At the time, they didn't appear that way, but looking back I realized some of my theories on love and relationships were based on my hatred of myself. I thought I was unworthy of love. So I didn't seek love, since I felt, inside, that no one could possibly want me. How could anyone else love me when I didn't even love myself?

I realized a lot of these feelings stemmed from my upbringing and situations that happened in my formative years. Now I understood that once I reached that realization, I could move forward. This summer I was able to face some of those ugly demons. And like Mama said, time heals all wounds. So Darius actually did me a favor. Now I was just counting down my time until my escape.

Since Mama had been hanging out with Mr. Peterson, he had cooked dinner for her at his house several nights in a row, and she hadn't noticed my distress. I was still getting used to our new, developing relationship, so I didn't burden her with the details of my relationship, or lack of relationship, with Darius. I simply told her that Darius and I had talked and it wasn't going to work out. Besides, I wasn't into long-distance relationships, and we were going our separate ways soon.

Mama just shook her head in dismay and said, "What a shame. That boy is gonna make somebody a good husband." I gave her one of my looks, and she shut up in a hurry.

I heard her whisper, "Well, he is."

I hung up with Shaneeka, who I was so proud of, and scooted off my bed and walked into the kitchen in my bare feet. I washed and put a few bowls and cups in the sink, checked out the refrigerator and tried to figure out what I could cook for dinner. I wasn't really hungry, but I figured cooking would at least take my mind off my problems.

The refrigerator didn't hold a lot to work with, but I couldn't get myself to go back to the grocery store to buy some more groceries. Every evening when I passed Piggly Wiggly, I thought of the face off with Darius. My hands would start to tremble and my heartbeat would speed up.

Thirty-six

I thought about it and realized I hadn't heard from or seen Redman since our so-called date. I had to smile because I knew he'd never change. However, I knew that I had grown, and I seriously doubted that we'd ever be together in a sexual manner again. I just hoped that we could remain friends. Maybe, one day soon, he'd meet a good woman who would settle him down and enable him to reach his potential.

Today, after work, I'd changed into some cutoff jeans shorts and a wife beater T-shirt and had my braids pulled back with a red bandanna around my head. Not exactly a glamorous picture; more like Florence the maid. It looked like I was going to have to cook some breakfast foods for dinner because that's about all I could dig up.

I took out a couple of eggs, some white bread for toast, half a pack of bacon and a small pot for grits. After filling up the pot with water and turning on the stove to medium-high, I walked into the living room to turn on the six o'clock evening news because the house was just too quiet. Gave me too much time to think. I needed a distraction.

So I had the news station blasting as the anchorwoman talked about the hot temperatures still ahead for the remainder of the week. Great! Because images of Darius kept popping into my mind, I had to catch myself as I cracked open eggs into the stainless-steel skillet. I really messed things up with him. Correction, we both messed up things up with each other. Sad. When I was honest with myself, I realized he was a good man. I guess I was so used to meeting the not so good ones that when I had a good one, I couldn't see it, or maybe I saw it and it scared me. Either way, he was out of my life.

I was so into my daydreaming that I didn't move to answer the doorbell until it had rung several times.

"Okay, okay. I'm coming."

Mama was always going out and forgetting to take her keys. I didn't know where that woman's mind was recently. I glanced down at my watch; it was still too early for her to arrive back home. She and Mr. Peterson were supposed to go out to dinner and a movie. As she was dressing for her date, she was as giddy as a teenager. I was starting to see a new side of her. A likable one.

I quickly turned down the flame on the stove as the doorbell rang again.

"Okay, hold your horses," I screamed, running and snatching open the front door without looking out the peephole. I was totally shocked to see Darius standing on the other side. We were face-to-face. Inches from each other. Yet so many barriers separated us.

In rapid breaths, Darius spoke first. "Mer, can I talk to you for a moment?"

I didn't say a word, but just looked on as if he had lost his damn mind. I wanted to say *Hell no. Get the fuck off my property.*

"I know I am the last person you expected to see after, after, the uh . . . other day, but I can't sleep, can't eat. I need to talk to you."

I motioned for him to come in. I couldn't trust my voice to speak. Emotions were swirling all over the place. I could barely see straight. And it was taking everything I had to just breathe.

"Have a seat, and let me turn off the stove. I was fixing some dinner." I shocked myself by acting civil when I should have been ranting and raving. See, I knew I was changing. Any other time and my ghetto-fabulous ways would be front and center.

"I'm sorry; I should have called first. But I knew if I did, you wouldn't see me."

"You're right on that one."

I quickly went into the kitchen and turned off my dinner. I grabbed the scarf off my head, patted down my hair and returned to the living room, where Darius stood, looking like a lost puppy.

"I'll return the favor. You have five minutes. Talk."

"Okay."

"Sit."

"No, no thanks," Darius said, looking nervously around at the wall, the floor, everywhere but at me.

"Listen, I'll make this short and sweet. That wasn't me the other day. I'm very sorry. So sorry."

"Well, it certainly looked like you to me. Do you have a twin that you didn't tell me about, as well?" I asked in the nastiest tone I could muster.

"The things I said and did, that wasn't me. My head wasn't on straight. I was trying to hurt you, to get back at you. You put a serious hurting on my ego and my heart . . . Please say that you'll find it in your heart to forgive me so that I can live with myself."

"Oh, so you drive over here and give me a bullshit-filled apology, and I'm suppose to smile and forgive you that easily?"

"Mer, all I can say is I'm sorry from the bottom of my heart. If you accept it or not, that's on you. At least I'll be able to sleep at night. I can't change what happened."

"All that stuff you said to me and the way you handled me. How could you, Darius?"

"I know it's not an excuse, but between your refusing to talk to me, my ex back in town, the emotion of seeing my daughter and then seeing you with that man at the grocery store, it was all too much," Darius said, plopping down on the sofa like he didn't have an ounce of energy left and putting his head in his hands.

At the mention of his ex, my curiosity got the best of me. "What's going on with your ex?"

"Supposedly Latrice has gotten her life back on track and came to town to make amends and to let me see my daughter."

I eased myself into the armchair beside the sofa where Darius was now sitting.

"Mer, I'm so tired of this entire mess. All my life all I ever wanted was a family. I'm serious. Other boys dreamed of cars, money, big houses. All I wanted was a wife, a couple of kids and a loving family life. I grew up without a father. Don't get me wrong, I had a loving childhood, but a woman, Mama, can't replace the nurture of a man to a boy. When I met my ex, I thought I could have it all. And we did for a while."

"Umph."

"I can't believe I haven't seen my daughter in almost a year. She's grown so much. I've missed so much."

"You're kidding? What happened?" I asked in disbelief and shock.

"Well, I've seen my daughter only on and off, the last few years, a couple of times. Latrice's parents kept her away. They went as far as to move to another state so that I wouldn't have easy access to my daughter."

"Why?"

"They blamed me for everything, for Latrice getting involved in drugs, for her being unhappy, everything. Blamed all that shit on me. Couldn't fathom the thought that picture-perfect Latrice did those horrible things all by herself. To herself. Then, when I lost everything, they came to me and said that they'd gladly keep Shelby until I got back on my feet. Of course, it was temporary. Before I knew it, my in-laws had sneaked and filed guardianship papers, had my daughter and soon moved to another state. Of course, my ex was too drugged up to know what was going on or to offer any help. At that point, Latrice didn't care. All she could think of was her next fix. And I never forgave her."

I sat there in disbelief. "And you couldn't tell me all this? Maybe I could have done something to help. Even if it was just to talk about it with you. Let you get out all that pent-up frustration."

"In the beginning, it didn't seem relevant for you to know about my past. I had told you I was once married. I figured that was all you needed to know, because talking about my daughter caused me too much pain. Then, as we got closer, I couldn't find the appropriate time to tell you because I knew how you felt about so-called baby mama drama. And, well, you know the rest."

"Man, that's deep. I didn't know."

"And you wouldn't let me explain."

"Are you okay now?"

"I'm taking it day by day. We are filing paperwork now for some sort of joint custody agreement. As far as I can tell, Latrice is off the crack, but she's still struggling to get back on her feet. It's gonna be a slow process."

"Darius, I'm so sorry. I didn't know. You should have confided in me. You didn't have to carry this all by yourself. I guess I was so into myself and what was going on in my household, I didn't sense your pain. Will you forgive me?"

"If you'll forgive me."

"Forgive you for all that shit you said about me? Hell no."

"Mer, you broke my heart. I hadn't felt that way since Latrice did her dirt. I didn't mean most of it."

"Oh, so you did mean some of it?"

"Well, baby, you don't appreciate yourself like you should, but know if I hadn't seen something great in you, I wouldn't have spent the majority of the summer with you. Wouldn't have wasted my time."

"Oh, really?"

"Yes, really."

With that, my face broke into a huge, genuine smile. As I walked to him, I held out my right hand for a handshake.

"It's a deal. I forgive you too. Now we're even."

"So what do we do now? This still isn't easy. Between the two of us, there are still so many problems and situations going on. Where do we go from here?"

"Let's just take it one step at a time and see where it leads. Let's take it slow," I offered, leaning against him. "Slow and easy.

"Since we are coming clean. There is something I need to tell you about my childhood."

"Sounds serious," Darius said, kissing my forehead.

"Yeah, it is. I guess you could say, I'm a product of a long-held secret. A secret that almost destroyed me."

"Mer, almost doesn't count."

"You're right, only counts in horseshoes."

"Well, nothing you could say could affect the way I feel about you at this moment. Mer, you are something else. I've always thought there was much more to you than meets the eye. My mama taught me that sometimes you have to dig beneath the surface."

"Well, let's eat and talk. It'll go down better with food."

"You mean you're going to cook me my first meal?" Darius asked with a silly smile on his face.

"Yeah, how do you like your eggs?" I asked, placing my finger in that dimple and planting a quick kiss on his cheek.

With that the mood was broken, and I knew we'd be okay. In fact, better than okay.

Over scrambled eggs, bacon, grits, toast and orange juice, I told Darius my story. And as expected, he didn't turn away from me or look at me any differently. All I saw was love and compassion radiating from his dark eyes. And anger against my molester. I cried again as I told my story. Cried for the abused and lonely child who somehow thought she created her situation. Cried for all the lonely, frightened nights that I spent huddled under my covers, wondering if it would happen that night. I cried for my innocence being taken away from me so early on. Even though I didn't know it at the time, I cried for something else that was lost along the way. My ability to completely love and trust again. My self-worth.

Looking into Darius's eyes and feeling his warm, strong, supportive embrace, gave me renewed hope for the future, our future. Darius held me as I cried and whispered loving and comforting words into my ears. He led me into the bathroom and made me look at the beautiful person I was, both inside and out. At first it was hard to look at myself in the mirror, but the more he whispered how beautiful I was, the more I believed him. For the first time, I really and truly believed him.

Darius told me the first day he saw me in the grocery store, he knew I was special and different. He had to have me. Own a piece of me. My spirit connected with his. Yeah, my man is deep and philosophical and I still have much to learn about him and from him. That night, he made me feel like the most loved and cherished person in the world.

After we jointly washed and dried the few dishes from the meal, which Darius went on and on about until I hit him with the wet dishrag, we watched some TV, enjoyed each other's company and fell asleep in each other's arms on the sofa. And that's how Mama found us a little after midnight.

"Ain't this a sight for sore eyes?"

"Mama?"

"Go back to sleep. I'm just spreading a blanket across you two. You're fine," she said with a sweet, genuine smile on her face. "Just fine."

"Thanks, Mama."

"Mer?"

"Yes, ma'am?"

"While you were sleeping, you looked so happy and peaceful. He's the one. I know he's the one," she whispered.

"I've been trying to tell your daughter that, Miss Jackson," Darius whispered back.

"Oh, no, you weren't playing possum?" I asked. Mama and I both burst into happy laughter, and I gently popped him upside his head.

"Y'all go back to sleep. I'm calling it a night myself. Love both of you."

"Good night," we both said in unison and drifted back to sleep in each other's arms.

Thirty-seven

For my remaining three weeks at home, Darius and I were inseparable. If you saw him, you saw me, and vice versa. Before and after work, we spent as much time together as possible. Some mornings we met for an early breakfast at Denny's before heading to work in our separate vehicles. Most evenings I greeted him as he walked through the door of his place with a prepared meal. Nothing fancy. When we finally did have sex again, Darius and I made love slowly and gently, and it felt so right. It wasn't about me getting off, but about me expressing my true feelings though intimacy. Skin to skin, heartbeat to heartbeat. I felt a magical and spiritual release rolled into one.

Believe it or not, Darius's mom and I get along much better. Mrs. Dargon told me that when she saw how our breakup made her son so unhappy, she realized how special I was to him and that I needed to be in his life. So through her love of cooking, we were slowly bonding. Mrs. Dargon showed me how to prepare some of Darius's favorite meals. I'm surprising even myself. Even though he hasn't said so, this bonding makes Darius very happy. Mrs. Dargon wasn't as bad as I thought she was. She could definitely grow on you.

One Sunday, we hung out with his daughter, Shelby. I was a little nervous at first. I hadn't really been around small children before, since I was an only child and didn't have any nieces or nephews. Our outing to the petting zoo started out awkwardly, but by the end of the day, all was well. Seeing Darius interact with his daughter just melted my heart, and I couldn't phantom how Latrice would want to keep Darius out of Shelby's life. Darius was a wonderful father. Very attentive and doting.

I think things changed between Shelby and I when she placed her tiny hand in mine and walked between her daddy and me. I felt an instant connection and couldn't believe that I thought she meant trouble or was baggage. I just wanted to protect her and see that precious smile. Shelby oohed and aahed at all the different animals. She saw ponies, sheep, horses, pigs, rabbits and could pet and feed them. A family standing near us commented what a beautiful child she was and thought I was her mother. I beamed. For one of the first times, I felt maternal stirrings within. I was learning new things about myself each and every day.

When Shelby fell and got a small scrape on her right knee and ran straight to me to fix it, with tears in her eyes, my heart leaped with joy. Being part of a family didn't seem foreign at all. It felt wonderful. The tiny peck she gave me on the cheek when we dropped her off with Darius's mom spoke volumes. I couldn't take my eyes or smile off her until she had merrily bounced her way into the house.

Even though we didn't talk about it, my time was almost over at Mama's house. My manager was releasing me in one week. Darius and I hadn't talked about what would happen after I left or made any plans for continuing our relationship long distance. It was like that was a taboo subject. So we just went on acting as if I wasn't going anywhere. Pretending. I was good at pretending. I had done it my entire life. Pretending everything was fine when it wasn't. It wasn't like I'd be a state away. Hell, I would only be four hours away from Darius. Four hours were nothing.

Yet I knew that once we returned to our separate lives, which consisted of jobs, friends and other commitments, things would change. Shaneeka and I lived a more hurried lifestyle in Atlanta; we partied. Now I was looking at things differently, but without Darius in my space, in my life in Atlanta, I wondered if I would backslide. And sex was very important to me. Would I drive four hours to get some because I realized Darius couldn't see me every weekend due to his job at UPS and joint custody of his daughter? Those were the questions that were left unspoken and unanswered during my final days.

Thirty-eight

My last night at home, Mama decided to treat everyone to dinner at a local buffet-style restaurant. As I sat at the large circular table next to Darius and watched her and Mr. Peterson interact, for the first time in a long time, I felt proud to call her my mom. It's amazing how a little forgiveness can work miracles in your life. Mama and I had come so far this summer. I realized how much I had missed her in my life and how much I truly needed her. Too many truths remained unspoken for too long. Sometimes the truth hurts, but sometimes it can set you free.

That's what I felt. For the first time in my life, I felt free. Free as a bird in flight. I remembered as a child I used to pray to God to give me wings so that I could fly far, far away. There were no longer any unspoken truths, dreams or nightmares that were secretly destroying me from the inside out. Everything had erupted to the top of the surface, and now the healing process had begun.

Sitting next to Darius, who was casually dressed in tan slacks and shirt, I felt almost complete as he lifted my hand to place a small kiss on the back of my wrist. Tiny moths fluttered inside my heart. I loved this man. I wanted to scream it at the top of my lungs. For the first time in my life, I felt connected to a man.

I could tell that Mr. Peterson was definitely taken with Mama. He was a few years older than her, but maybe that's what she needed to slow her down some. They had been neighbors for many years, but had never noticed each other. Or at least, Mama didn't notice him. It's amazing how sometimes God forces you to stop. Be it physically or emotionally. And then you have no choice but to observe your surroundings. It took Mama's knee surgery for them to hook up.

Last night, Mama and I really talked again. As I lay on the sofa in my pj's with my head in her lap, we talked like old friends, like mother and daughter.

"Mer, I'm gonna miss you, child."

"I can't believe I'm saying this, but I'm gonna miss you too."

"Thanks. I guess that's a compliment. I'll take it. I know I don't say this often, but I'm proud of you, baby."

"Thank you, Mama," I said, my eyes tearing up. I don't think I had ever heard her say that before.

"I know that your childhood wasn't a bed of roses, but you survived and grew into a strong, beautiful lady. You're still standing. But I'm hoping that you'll let Darius be the provider of some of that strength. A pillar to lean on."

I nodded my head. In reality, I still didn't know where Darius and I were headed. We still had a long road full of detours and forks to travel.

"When you get home, don't forget me. Call me, and let's continue to develop this new relationship. Let's talk at least once a week. And don't you ever forget that never for one minute have I ever stopped loving you, Mer."

"I won't."

"I know we can't change the past, but now we are going to focus on our future. Okay?"

"Okay."

"And, Mer, I know you get upset when I meddle, but I really

like Darius. He's a good man, and I can tell that he loves you. I mean, the man loves you even when you have one foot out the door. You're finally free, baby, and what was missing for you, you found it in Darius."

"You may be right," I said, a smile lighting up my face like lights on a Christmas tree.

"Don't grow old, bitter and alone like I have."

"Doesn't look like you're going to be alone for long, if Mr. Peterson has anything to say about it."

"He does kind of adore me, doesn't he?"

"Yeah, you could say that," I said, and I believe I saw Mama blush for the first time.

"Makes me wonder if I'll ever look at another woman again."

"Mama, you are too much."

"And you know it."

We both laughed.

"Mer, I've never been very honest or verbal with my feelings. Even though I may not have said it all the time or showed it, I've always loved you, and I love you so very much today."

"I love you too."

"We received a second chance to renew our mother-daughter relationship."

"Let's do the damn thang." We both laughed.

As the clinking glass brought me out of my reverie, I looked around and all eyes were on me. Darius squeezed my hand under the table. I squeezed back.

"If I can get my daughter to stop daydreaming, I'd like to say grace."

We proceeded to hold hands and lower our heads in prayer.

"Dear Heavenly Father, we come here today in peace and filled to the brim with the goodness that you've bestowed upon us. You've brought the people at this table together for a reason, for your divine purpose. This is our season. Help us learn to appreciate that it's never too late to seek forgiveness or give it. That's one of the great lessons in life. Bless my daughter, God. Bring her inner peace and happiness. Bless this young man who came into her life at a time when she needed him. Keep them strong through this separation period, but let them know that love conquers all. Bestow your blessings on my friend, my neighbor, and keep him in your good graces. And finally, Lord, show me how to be a true mother, friend and confidante to my daughter. Help us make up for lost time and put the past behind us and realize that it's just that . . . the past. It's a time for new beginnings. As the flowers bloom in spring, I pray that our relationship will blossom like a spring bouquet. All these things we ask in your name, Jesus. Amen and thank God."

"Amen and thank God," we all spoke in unison.

I saw Darius give me the eye like he didn't know Mama could get down like that with God. There were many things I was also still learning about my mom, and vice versa. And believe it or not, I couldn't wait to find out more. Mama and I decided that we'd seek therapy to work out or talk out our past. Mama suggested it to me, and at first I resisted the idea, but the more I thought about it, the more I thought I deserved to be happy, and working with a professional was a start in the right direction towards obtaining it.

The remainder of dinner was full of good cheer, laughter and love. It was odd seeing Mama in action with Mr. Peterson. Through all their antics, I could sense a feeling of love, respect and caring between them. You never knew when love would come into your life. And I have to admit, Mama's new clothes and fresh haircut were very flattering. I knew she'd be fine once I left; Mr. Peterson would see to that. At one point she saw me staring at her. She looked at me and winked. I winked back.

After dessert and coffee, I left knowing that one summer had changed my life. For the better. Forever. One summer.

Once we arrived back home, Mr. Peterson gave me a fatherly hug and told me to take care and to not be a stranger. I respected him so much, because a few days earlier, he had paid me a visit at work, taken me out to lunch, to Morrison Cafeteria, and professed how much he loved my mama. He looked so cute in his khaki pants and shirt.

"Mer, I'm very aware of your mother's past and dealings with women, but we can't help who we fall in love with. Only the heart knows."

I started to open my mouth to speak, and he shushed me so that he could continue. I listened; he talked.

"I know the neighbors and this town are talking about our relationship. I'm too old to care. And you know what? I don't care, because I love your mama. I wasted too many years watching and waiting for her to notice me. I learned that sometimes you have to make life happen. If you keep waiting, it just may pass you by."

"I'm happy for you, sir. I know how Mama can be. She's not the easiest person to love, but I'm glad you've found it."

"Well, yeah. I'm just thrilled that she's happy again. I've lived next door to her for so many years and always sensed a deep unhappiness that she tried to hide. Never knew where it came from. But now it's like a veil has been lifted from a heavy heart. She knew how to love; she just needed someone to bring it out. Nurture it."

"You may be right."

"And, Mercedes, you keep seeking your happiness. Don't give up on it, baby girl. It's there, right in front of you, waiting for you to claim it. Take it for what it is, and don't ever think that you're not deserving. No one is perfect."

"I will."

"Don't say you will. Just reach out and grab it. Take it, claim it, darling. You, your mama, y'all are always in my prayers."

"Don't wait to be an old woman to find your happiness when it's already staring you in the face."

"You are so right."

"Years from now, you don't want regrets or to hear yourself saying, *I almost*. You know what they say?"

"No. What?"

"Sugar, almost doesn't count."

Again, my mind wandered back to the here and now. Mama said good night and quickly retired to her room. That left Darius and me alone. We had already decided that there would be no sad, prolonged good-byes. In fact, there wouldn't be any good-byes. We decided to sorta play it by ear and see what happens. That's how our situation was left. If we were meant to be together, then it would happen. He had my number and I had his.

"Well, I guess this is it," Darius said, reaching for my hand. He gave a gentle squeeze. We were still sitting in the living room.

"Yeah, I guess so. I had a wonderful evening," I said, leaning into Darius and giving him a tight hug. I wasn't ready to say good night.

"Me too."

"Well, Mer, I'm not going to stay long because I know you have an early start to a long drive in the morning. You need your sleep. Wouldn't want you falling asleep on the road."

"Okay."

When he pulled me to my feet, he whispered, "Come here."

"Okay."

"You know how I feel about you. I love you, but I know we need to take this slow," he said, gently rubbing my back and pulling me into an easy embrace.

I didn't say anything. I just looked at the floor. It was still hard for me to acknowledge my feelings for Darius. I guess there was a part of me that was still afraid of being hurt. This was all so new to me. I was still learning.

Darius pulled my chin back up. "Did you hear me? I love you, Mer."

"I know."

"There's that hesitation from a heart that's not really sure," Darius kidded, but I saw the hint of hurt flash quickly away.

"I'm very sure."

"I'm glad, because almost doesn't count."

"I'm sure, baby. We'll see what happens," I said in all seriousness.

"Listen, let me go. I could stay here all night holding you. Have a safe drive, think of me, and I'll call you."

I just nodded my head as I walked him to the front door, my hand in his. We hugged one more time as our lips and mouths hungrily found each other. I didn't want to let go. I wanted to hold on to him forever.

"What time are you leaving?"

"Six a.m."

"Okay, I'll think of you at that moment."

"That's sweet. Good night, baby," I said, leaning forward for a kiss.

"Good night. Man, I'm going to miss you," he said, backing away from the door and walking slowly to his black truck. He looked back several times.

"I'll miss you more," I whispered to the wind.

After I watched him drive away, I slowly closed the door and leaned against it. For a moment, an overpowering sadness enveloped me. That night, before retiring to my bed, I did something I hadn't done since I was a little girl. I said my prayers, and I asked God to release my inability to totally give my heart to someone. I didn't want to lead Darius on and let him down. He didn't deserve that.

Thirty-nine

The next morning came before I knew it. My alarm clock abruptly pulled me from a delicious dream I was having of me and Darius. I'm glad I had packed everything into my car the night before. After I took a quick shower and dressed, Mama surprised me with a small breakfast of country ham, grits and orange juice before I left.

Not much was said at breakfast. We sat in a comfortable silence. Man, we had come a long way. We basked in the renewed love that we felt for each other. Mama told me her plans of going back to work in another two weeks or so. We recommitted to calling each other at least once a week. When it was time to leave, I told her it wasn't necessary for her to walk me out since the car was already packed. We hugged at the door, said I love yous and that was that. I could have sworn I saw tears glistening in Mama's eyes.

At the last minute, I checked the house one final time, took my time going from room to room, and then headed out the door with one final hug for Mama. Once I made it to my car, I sat there and stared back at the house for a few minutes. I didn't want to leave. It's funny how that house would now hold new and wonderful memories for me. I finally drove off with a sense of fleeting sadness, but with a renewed sense of strength.

I wondered if I should have taken the bank up on their offer.

Even though I didn't tell Mama or Darius, the bank manager had offered me a full-time position there. It seemed my hard work and dedication had paid off. Many of my customers had sent letters to the manager complimenting my work and customer service. Even my coworkers looked sad to see me go. They threw me a going-away party complete with cake and punch. Who would have thought?

As it stood, I had an open invitation for employment there. It was so tempting to say yes, but I knew I owed it to myself to find myself first. Darius's words were still in the back of my mind. *You need to learn to love yourself first. Discover your worth.* I intended to do just that. It was the only way I could make peace with myself and be an asset for someone else. I needed to love myself before I could completely love someone else.

I was already in daydream mode when a loud car horn brought me back to reality. I put on my blinkers when I saw Darius pull up beside me and signal for me to pull over. I slowly pulled over by the sidewalk, got out of my car and quickly walked towards him.

"Darius?"

"I thought I had missed you, Mer."

"Darius, what are you doing here?" I asked with confusion on my face. "I thought we had decided . . ."

"I tossed and turned all last night. The entire time, I wanted you by my side, in my arms. I probably got two good hours of sleep. This morning, I had to see you, to say good-bye. To say good-bye for now, anyway. I had to look into your pretty face one more time."

"Darius, you are making this hard," I said, holding back tears. "Very hard."

"I know, baby, but I can't live without you in my life. I realize you have to find your place in the world first. I know that. I understand that."

"You're going to make me cry."

"Don't, baby. I don't want you to be sad. This is a time to rejoice. I want you to be happy knowing that I'm always on your side. I got your back. No matter what. Here, I have this for you."

"What is it?" I asked, looking at a small gift-wrapped box.

"Just open it, please."

"Okay." I quickly opened the gold box to reveal a small gold key, the kind you see on charm bracelets.

"That's the key to my heart. When you are ready to use it, let me know. I'm not giving up on you, on us. I want you to be a permanent part of my life, every day, but I know it won't work until you are ready to make that commitment. Now, I'm not going to wait forever, but this is our symbol. I'm totally and completely caught up."

I was speechless. "I love you!" I couldn't believe my ears. I screamed it this time. "I love you, Darius."

"What? Say it again. That's the first time you've ever said that. That's music to my ears."

"I know, but I mean it, with all my heart. I love you, baby."

"You are something else."

Wrapped in each other, Darius and I held each other for a few more minutes. Gazing into each other's eyes. Unable to let go. Unwilling to let go. Reluctantly, Darius walked me back to my car as I wiped away a few tears of happiness.

"Go on. Get in before somebody calls the police on two idiots standing in the middle of the road crying and screaming. They'd swear we were trying to rob somebody's house."

"Bye, baby."

"Not bye, but later," he said, pushing a loose braid out of my face. "I miss you already."

"I miss you more," I whispered.

With that Darius walked back to his car. As I drove by, he mouthed that he'd call me tonight.

I mouthed back. "You'd better."

Epilogue

Almost a year later . . .

The young girl awoke to the sun shining brightly into her bedroom. Someone had opened the sheer curtains to reveal the start of a beautiful morning. The birds were chirping in the trees, and she could hear the everyday patter of families getting ready for their everyday, ordinary lives. Laughter filled the air.

This morning felt different. There was no dread or fear or shame that the night after usually brought forth. Today there was a pep to her step, a gleam in her eyes and a smile on her face. She carefully set Sweetmouth to the side and informed her old friend and confidante that she wouldn't need her anymore. It was time to move on.

As the young girl rose from the bed, a funny and miraculous thing happened. As she placed first one foot and then the other firmly on the floor and made her way to the small dresser mirror by the wall, she grew up in front of her own eyes. The woman before her was confident, attractive, bright and had a sense of peace in her heart. The face that looked back bore the telltale signs of life and living, sorrow and defeat, joys and triumphs, but today that face glowed in self-love. The kind of radiant love that told the world "I love myself even if no one else does. Treat me with respect, dignity and grace because I am worthy of your love. Within my bosom I possess all the qualities that make me so deserving. I now know the secret to achieving a woman's worth." She found herself humming some of the lines of a popular Alicia Keys song. *"A real man knows a real woman when he sees her. A real man just can't deny a woman's worth."*

The woman with the long braids pulled back off her face reached into her velvet jewelry box and pulled out a gold charm bracelet that had about ten gold charms on it. However, she focused on one. The charm that was in the shape of a gold key.

The time had finally come. The day she had been living and breathing for. All the hurts of the past were gone, pushed so far back that they were invisible now. Joy really did come in the morning. Her heart was wide open to receive love and family and happiness. The woman deserved it. Today was the day she claimed the key to his heart.

A Note from the Author

Dear Readers,

Before I go any further, I'd like to thank you guys and give my sincere appreciation for all the e-mails, letters and positive reviews I receive; it warms my heart to no end. I can be having one of those "pity party" days and hear from one of you and I realize that I'm fulfilling my purpose. Your validation pulls me back into focus.

Whew! I can't believe this is book number three! Thanks so much for accompanying me on yet another wild roller coaster ride, full of ups and downs, highs and lows, steep curves and valleys, smooth paths and gravel roads; much like real life. I hope you held on tight and enjoyed the ride. Mercedes is going to be just fine because she's a survivor!

I still have to pinch myself now and again to make sure I'm not dreaming. I'm living out a dream . . . writing full-time. Who would have thought that I'd make the transition from print on demand (POD) to self-published to mainstream author? From corporate America to full time writer? Me . . . I thought it, pursued it and most of all claimed it! That's right, ask and you shall receive . . . claim your destiny! Shout it to the universe!

I don't want to feel like I'm preaching (LOL), but I want readers to understand that it's never, ever, too late to follow your dreams

and truly live your life to the fullest. Life is too short . . . and unfortunately we don't receive a dress rehearsal. Here and now . . . this
is the real deal.

Readers have asked what motivates me to write about dysfunctional characters in steamy, drama-filled relationships? Simple answer: because they exist. For those of you who know a little about
me, you know I'm a realist and a true observer of life. I try to keep
it real. Everybody doesn't have the "ideal" relationship or marriage.
In fact, most people don't have that type of relationship; look at the
divorce statistics in the U.S.

My main characters are the true underdogs in our society;
everyone isn't a Black African Princess (BAP), earning a high pay-
ing six-figure salary, or involved in "picture perfect" relationships. I
applaud those stories/books that focus on healthy and striving relationships; I'm in one.

However, on the flip side of that coin, I write where my muse
leads me, because there are women who are totally confused (mis-
construing sex for love), hopelessly trapped (in unhealthy relationships and repeating the same cycles over and over again),
conveniently settling (for men who will never change or who
aren't compatible to them), sexually repressed and/or very open-
minded (due to misinformation/moral issues or willing to experi-
ment and understanding that women have strong sexual appetites)
and not loving themselves (low self-esteem issues).

Women need to empower themselves: mind, body and spirit.
We need to accept the fact that many of us will never marry; will
never find a soul mate. However, a relationship or marriage
shouldn't define who you are. Love yourself first. Quit wasting
your life and time searching for Mr. Right or trying to turn someone into him. When and if the universe is ready for you to find

him, you will. I'm a firm believer that everything happens for a reason and in its own time. It's all predestined.

Bottom line, I will continue to be the voice of those characters whose stories haven't always been represented and hopefully, you will continue to read them. Unfortunately, every story doesn't have a happily ever after ending, but they shouldn't be ignored.

Please continue to share your feedback with me; keep me on my toes, but remember I'm sensitive now (LOL). Until our next drama-filled, sensual journey together, take care.

Much love,
Electa

Almost ⊙ ⊙ ⊙

Doesn't Count

Electa Rome Parks

A CONVERSATION WITH
ELECTA ROME PARKS

Q. What can you tell your readers about Electa Rome Parks?

A. Umm, that's a hard question. It's not easy to define or describe one's self in a condensed version, but I'll try. I was born and raised in Georgia. So yes, I'm a true Georgia peach even though I lived in Chicago and North Carolina for many years. Basically, I'm just your average, down to earth, wife and mother of two who has a great passion for writing and reading. Honestly, I don't think I could live without books and the written word. I've found that a pen to paper is a powerful tool!

Let's see, what else can I divulge about myself and keep you interested (smile)? Believe it or not, I'm actually kinda quiet and laid back. I can be moody and oversensitive (Pisces trait). So . . . be careful what you say about *Almost Doesn't Count* because I'm sensitive about my stuff (LOL).

I have a very vivid imagination that is evident in my books and I believe in a lot of theories that most people would think bizarre. Let's just say I absolutely love *X-Files* and the entire concept of spirits, spirit guides, guardian angels, and karma. I once had a palm reader tell me I was a writer in another life and that's why writing validates and elevates me to be in complete sync with my spirit. I thought that was so profound and so unbelievably true.

Bottom line, anyone who truly knows me will state that I'm real. I'm very approachable and have a genuine caring nature (another Pisces trait). I have my "few" imperfections (i.e., control freak, temper tantrums and impatience to name a few) and struggles just like the next person. However, I believe in order to really get in touch with our true spirit, we need to discover our gifts. I feel that we are all born into the world with a special gift and I've found mine. That brings me great joy!

What else? I pretty much suck at any sport, my favorite color is purple, I've never weighted more than 112 pounds my entire life, my all-time favorite movie is a toss between *Soul Food* and *The Best Man* and I have tons of stories to share with my readers.

Q: What do you want people to come away with after reading your novels?

A: Primarily, I'm writing for entertainment value first. I write for the readers who want a mini-vacation without ever leaving the sanctuary of their home. I write for that reader who on a cold, wintry day, wants nothing other than to curl up under a warm afghan in front of a toasty fireplace, sip on some hot tea, and read about somebody else's life. Not just read about it, but get pulled in, engulfed by it and feel the pure emotion. Feel the heat!

If readers take something away in the process, then that's great too; that's an added bonus. I've accomplished my goal and much more; it makes it all worthwhile.

Every time I feel like giving up because the publishing industry is too stressful or the monsters (insecurity, impatience and doubt) have reared their ugly heads, I receive an e-mail or a personal letter from an avid reader and it makes my day to realize I've made an impact on somebody's life. I can't describe that feeling.

Q: *Why do you think your writing is so well received?*

A: I'm an avid reader myself and I know what is entertaining for me to read. I feel that if readers crave elements of high drama, exciting relationships, smothering spiciness, more drama, compelling characters, and added twists and turns, then they'll embrace my books, which they have.

Also, with the correct blending of elements, I feel my books come across as real, i.e., my characters are ordinary people who are going through realistic "episodes" in their every day life that readers can relate to in one way or the other.

Q: *Okay, you know folks are nosey when it comes to celebrities. Tell us what it's like being Electa Rome Parks? What does your day consist of?*

A: What's it like being Electa Rome Parks? Readers, by the way, my first name is Electa, not Electra (LOL). That is such a pet peeve of mine because I've gone my entire life with people calling me Electra, Electricity, Electron, etc. I remember back in middle school when . . . (LOL). Man, I kinda got off the topic on that one. Sorry (smile).

First of all, I definitely wouldn't classify myself as a celebrity! But, my day is pretty basic and boring; nothing out of the ordinary here. Since I now work full time as a writer, I try to remain disciplined and balanced. For those of you who know a little about me, that's easier said than done.

A typical day goes something like this: After dropping off my children at elementary school and picking up breakfast at Chick Fil-A (I love their biscuits and sodas), I head home, sign onto my PC and check and respond to e-mails first.

Then, I'll usually check out some of the yahoo groups and see what's going on in the literary industry that may be of interest to me. Finally, if I'm working on a project, I'll get the creative juices flowing by re-reading what I've written the day before, focusing on my characters, and channeling in on their voices. Then it's on.

Around one o'clock or so, I break for lunch, run errands to my post office box, do mail outs, and return phone calls, etc. I arrive back and continue writing some more until my kids arrive home on the school bus. Once they are here, we chat and eat a snack, then I re-check e-mails, write some more and eventually call it a day no later than six o'clock. However, the problem is that my working mode never cuts off. So, I can find myself back on my PC in my hustle mode throughout the remainder of the evening and night.

I'm absolutely obsessed. Weekends are filled with book signings, book club meetings and other literary events.

(Stop yawning.) See, I told you my days were pretty boring. This year, I'm going to attempt to write my next manuscript on my newly purchased laptop. This way I can get away from the house, go the library or wherever, and see other human faces and not have my desktop as an extension of my body (LOL).

Q: What has been the most gratifying part of being an author?

A: Hands down, the most gratifying part of being an author has been meeting and greeting new and interesting readers who are embracing my stories and e-mailing me and writing me and meeting me at signings and telling me how much they've enjoyed my books! We talk about my characters like they are old friends. No matter how many times I've experienced that, it always makes my day. Puts a big Kool-Aid smile on my face (LOL).

Their (the reader's) feedback and reactions totally validate that my craft is a gift from God! If I can touch a number of people with my stories or even if I only entertain them and they don't walk away with a life lesson, then I've still done my job.

As you know, my stories are typically relationship based, very drama filled with an ounce of spice thrown in, well maybe a pound of spice thrown in, and they usually cover a topical issue that is prevalent in today's society. Believe me, I have so many characters screaming inside my head, waiting to tell their story, that I feel like the lady from the movie Sybil (LOL). So, bottom line, I pray and claim that my readership base will continue to grow and I'll have wonderful opportunities to meet many more fans.

Q: *Where do you see yourself as a writer ten years from now?*

A: It's all about continuing to elevate myself to the next level. There's always room for growth and improvement. Ten years from now, I'd love to see myself as a full-time writer entertaining my readers with fabulous, refreshing, dramatic stories of love, life and relationships. It's not about the money; it's all about the passion and joy you feel with each and every heartfelt word that turns into a sentence, then a paragraph, and eventually a completed novel. Being a writer is like being a creator of life . . . like giving birth. What can be better than that?

Q: *How do you define success?*

A: Good question. Personally, I define success as being able to do something you truly love on a day to day basis, getting paid for it in the process, giving back to the community (to whom much is given, much is expected) and being the best person you can be which enables you to sleep peacefully at night. To me, those combined elements make you a successful person. And . . . if you place God and your family first, the sky's the limit!

Q: *How do you deal with adversity and failure?*

A: I stress out! I totally freak out, have a pity party, and take to my bed (LOL)! I'm laughing, but I'm pretty accurate. I'm so hard on myself; I'm my worst critic, and I've got to stop doing that. I can't enjoy my successes because I'm too busy worrying about what I could have done better or thinking about the next venture.

After I finally pull myself out of bed and stop my pity party (this usually lasts for roughly twenty-four hours), I analyze my situation like I'm breaking down a trigonometry problem. After all is said and done, I learn the lesson, file it in my permanent memory bank, remember I'm still standing and move on. In afterthought, life lessons are wonderful, even the ones filled with adversity and failure; they make us stronger and wiser and who we are today.

Also, if I may add, I have a good support team in place with my family and friends. Plus, I have a solid spiritual foundation that keeps me strong and undaunted by the dream dashers.

Q: Has there been a significant life lesson for you?

A: A significant life lesson was my mom dying of breast cancer back in 1997. Her death at age fifty-two (my dad died at thirty-two) made me realize and appreciate how short and precious life truly is. After her death, I made the commitment then and there that I'd follow my dreams because I didn't know what tomorrow held. People are so caught up on playing it safe, sound and conservative; much can be said for that. Unfortunately, sometimes we look up and our lives have passed us by in the blink of an eye and all we can say is "what if." I don't want to ever have to ask myself "what if."

Q: *What do you do to stay grounded and maintain a sense of balance in your life?*

A: By spirit, I'm a pretty grounded person, but yet, a person with a negative aura can throw my system totally off. I'm very perceptive and can pick up on and take in people's energies fairly easily. I try to distance myself from negative people (you know who you are) and their damaging energies; however, when I find myself losing my sense of balance I do several things. I meditate to clear my mind (I always picture myself near water because water centers me), I pray to God for guidance and strength, and I talk to myself. Yes, I talk to myself, but not in a "crazy" way (LOL). I give myself little pep talks and cheer myself on.

QUESTIONS FOR DISCUSSION

1. Was Mercedes in control of her life or was she actually completely out of control?

2. What did you think of Merecedes's theories on men? On women? Were they valid?

3. Do you know any women with Mercedes's mentality?

4. What were your thoughts on Miss Betty? Did she love Mercedes?

5. What do you think of the friendship Mercedes and Shaneeka shared?

6. What was your opinion of Redman? What was your opinion of Jamal? Were they a lost cause?

7. What did Darius see in Mercedes that she couldn't see in herself? What attracted Darius to Mercedes? Was their relationship realistic?

8. Should Darius have been upfront about Shelby and Latrice? Why did he lie?

9. Did your impression of Darius change after what happened at his house when Mercedes went to apologize?

10. What were your thoughts on the deep dark secret? Were you shocked by the twist? Can these types of secrets destroy families?

11. Was Mercedes capable of loving Darius?

12. At the end of the book, do you feel Mercedes and Darius could ever have a lasting relationship? Where do you see them five years from now?